SUPER GENIUS
ASTRONOMY QUIZ

SUPER GENIUS ASTRONOMY QUIZ

DILIP M. SALWI

RUPA

To
Sumati P. Tawde
for her pious and
helpful nature

Dillip M. Salwi © Rupa & Co. 2004

First Published 2005
Fourth Impression 2012

Published by
Rupa Publications India Pvt. Ltd.
7/16, Ansari Road, Daryaganj
New Delhi 110 002

Sales Centres:

Allahabad Bengaluru Chennai
Hyderabad Jaipur Kathmandu
Kolkata Mumbai

Hello, Astronomy Buffs!

'1000 Astronomy & Space Quiz' has been in print for more than a decade now. So, when my publisher suggested me to produce two books out of this, I thought of separating astronomy from space. As a result, you have this book 'Super Genius Astronomy Quiz' in your hands. It was difficult to say which subject – astronomy or space – was more popular and what was the reason for slow yet steady sale of the book. But now, things will become clearer as quiz books on astronomy and space are now separate. Let me wait and watch.

I must make it very clear that nothing much revolutionary has happened in astronomy in the last decade except the discovery of planets around a large number of stars. Actually, it is a very exciting discovery as it has opened a Pandora's box of questions to which we want answers: for instance, are there earth-like planets in the universe; if so, has life evolved there? if yes, has intelligence evolved there; and if that is so, is there any civilisation there. I am sure in the years to come, some light will be thrown on these questions, making astronomy a much more exciting subject. This quiz book exclusively devoted to the subject will, I am sure, stimulate interest and create a love for the subject. Happy quizzing!

August 25, 2003

Dilip M. Salwi

Acknowledgements

I am thankful to the following persons and organisations for supplying me photographs published in the book: Asok K. Samanta, Manager, Archives, American Center, New Delhi; Malti Jai Kumar and Ravi Datta of the British Information Services, New Delhi. Indian Institute of Astrophysics, Bangalore; U.P. State Observatory; Astronomy Department of Osmania University; Saha Institute of Nuclear Physics and Dinesh Sinha. Last but not the least I am thankful to my wife Smriti, daughter Neha and son Romel for bearing with me while I was revising and updating this book.

Dilip M. Salwi

CONTENTS

I

FIRST THINGS FIRST

First Astronomers

1. Who was the first to provide evidence for the expansion of the universe?
   - (a) Harlow Shapley
   - (b) Henrietta S. Leavitt
   - (c) Henry Russell
   - (d) Edwin P. Hubble

2. Who was the first in the world to claim that the earth rotates about its axis and gave the correct rate of its rotation?
   - (a) Hipparchus
   - (b) Meton
   - (c) Ahmose
   - (d) Aryabhata I

3. Who was the first to explain the presence of dark lines in the sun's spectrum?
   - (a) Meghnad Saha
   - (b) Joseph von Fraunhofer
   - (c) Robert Bunsen
   - (d) Gustav Kirchhoff

4. Who was the first woman astronomer in recorded history?
   (a) Annie J. Cannon   (b) Henrietta S. Leavitt
   (c) Caroline Herschel   (d) Jocelyn Bell

5. Who was the first to compile a catalogue of star clusters and nebulae?
   (a) William Herschel   (b) J.L.E Draper
   (c) Charles Messier   (d) Annie J. Cannon

6. Who was the first to forward enough observations and data to support the view that the earth and other planets go around the sun?
   (a) Nicolaus Copernicus
   (b) Aristarchus
   (c) Claudius Ptolemy   (d) Tycho Brahe

7. Who was the first to observe way back in 1631 the transit of a planet across the face of the sun?
   (a) Johann Kepler   (b) Pierre Gassendi
   (c) Michael Mastlin   (d) Johann Bayer

8. Who was the first to build a radio telescope?
   (a) Karl Jansky   (b) Bernard Lovell
   (c) Grote Reber   (d) Henrik van de Hulst

9. Who was the first to photograph a double star?
   (a) Fred Whipple   (b) Lewis Rutherford
   (c) J.C Kapteyn   (d) George Phillips Bond

10. Who was the first to estimate how far a star is by measuring the parallax?
    (a) Friedrich W. Bessel   (b) Joseph von Fraunhofer
    (c) John Flamsteed   (d) F.G.W. Struve

11. Who was the first to identify a double radio source?
    (a) R.C. Jennison   (b) M.K. Das Gupta
    (c) J.S Hey   (d) Grote Reber

12. Who was the first to coin the name 'black hole' for an exotic and bizarre heavenly body?
    (a) Roger Penrose   (b) John Wheeler
    (c) Kip S. Thorne   (d) Karl Schwarzschild

First Things

13. Which was the first star to have its parallax and distance directly measured?
    (a) 61 Cygni   (b) Wolf 359
    (c) Procyon A   (d) Proxima Centauri

14. Which was the first white dwarf to be discovered?
    (a) Kuiper's star   (b) Sirius B
    (c) 40 Eridani B   (d) Procyon B

15. Which was the first heavenly body where active volcanoes were found?
    (a) Moon   (b) Io
    (c) Europa   (d) Saturn

16. Which was the first quasar – quasi-stellar object – to be discovered?
    (a) 3C-273   (b) PKS 2000-330
    (c) OX-169   (d) OQ 172

17. Which was the first compound reflecting telescope?
    (a) Newtonian telescope
    (b) Cassegrain telescope
    (c) Gregorian telescope
    (d) Schmidt telescope

18. Which comet was the first to encounter a spacecraft designed to study it?
    (a) Halley   (b) Kohoutek
    (c) Giacoboni-Zinner   (d) Biela

19. Which was the first 'modern' planet?
    (a) Uranus   (b) Neptune
    (c) Pluto   (d) Mars

20. Which was the first double star to be discovered?
    (a) Mizar   (b) Arcturus
    (c) Menkar   (d) Algedi

21. Which was the first comet in recorded history that broke into two between its first appearance and return?
    (a) Comet Alcock
    (b) Comet Bennett
    (c) Comet Kohoutek
    (d) Comet Biela

22. Where was the world's first modern planet-arium installed?
    (a) London
    (b) Moscow
    (c) New York
    (d) Bonn

23. Which was the first eclipsing binary star to be discovered?
    (a) Beta Lyrae
    (b) Algol
    (c) Epsilon Aurigae
    (d) Alpha Capricorni

24. Which was the first X-ray source that was discovered outside the solar system?
    (a) Scorpius X-1
    (b) Taurus X-1
    (c) Hercules X-1
    (d) Centaurus X-3

25. Where has the first planet-sized body been found orbiting the main star?
    (a) Proxima Centauri
    (b) Sirius
    (c) Van Bies Broeck-8
    (d) Beta Pictoris

26. Which was the first heavenly body with an extra solar planet discovered?
    (a) Quasar
    (b) Supernova
    (c) Pulsar
    (d) Brown Dwarf

II

PIONEERS AND INVENTORS

Pioneers

27. Who estimated the minimum distance at which a natural satellite can move around its planet without being torn apart?
    - (a) E.A. Roche
    - (b) J.E. Bode
    - (c) S.B. Nicholson
    - (d) G.P. Kuiper

28. Who predicted the presence of 'Brown Dwarf – the intermediate between a star and a planet – before it was eventually discovered?
    - (a) Chushiro Hayashi
    - (b) Victor Safronov
    - (c) Shiv Kumar
    - (d) Fred Hoyle

29. Who found the relationship between the absolute brightness of a star and its spectral class or temperature?
    - (a) James Jeans
    - (b) Ejnar Hertzsprung
    - (c) Arthur S. Eddington
    - (d) Henry Norris Russell

30. Who correctly predicted that the rings of Saturn were not solid but consisted of small particles?
    (a) Christan Huygens   (b) J.C. Maxwell
    (c) Johann Kepler   (d) Galieo Galilei

31. Who was the founder of lunar topography?
    (a) Johannes Hevelius   (b) Giovanni Riccioli
    (c) Johann Kepler   (d) Galileo Galilei

32. Whose equations predicted the existence of black holes from Albert Einstein's General Theory of Relativity?
    (a) S. Chandrasekhar   (b) Arthur S. Eddington
    (c) Karl Schwarzschild (d) James Jeans

33. Who dethroned the sun from the previously assumed position of the centre of our galaxy and gave a true picture of it?
    (a) J.C. Kapteyn   (b) J.H. Oort
    (c) Harlow Shapley   (d) Ernst Opik

34. Whose mathematical prediction of Neptune eventually led to its discovery?
    (a) J.C. Adams   (b) John Herschel
    (c) Friedrich W. Bessel (d) Urbain Leverrier

35. Who set up the pioneering experiment to detect neutrinos coming from the sun?
    (a) Wolfgang Pauli
    (b) Victor F. Hess
    (c) M.G.K. Menon
    (d) Raymond Davis

36. Who devised a scale of 'seeing' the state of atmosphere for astronomical observations?
    (a) John Dalton
    (b) Anders Celsius
    (c) E.M. Antoniadi
    (d) Nicolas Lacaille

37. Who estimated that the phases of the Moon occur on the same day of the month after every 19 years?
    (a) Johann Kepler
    (b) Meton
    (c) Galileo Galilei
    (d) Sosigenes

Pathfinders

38. Who showed that 'solar wind', a stream of highly energetic and charged particles, emitted by the sun exists?
    (a) Herbert Friedman
    (b) H.D. Babcock
    (c) Edward Maunder
    (d) E.N. Parker

39. Who forwarded the law that gives the mean distance of planets from the sun?
    (a) J.E. Bode
    (b) Johann Kepler
    (c) Tycho Brahe
    (d) Christiaan Huygens

40. Who asked the simple question, 'Why is the night dark?' and gave birth to a paradox?
    (a) J.P.L. Chesaux   (b) J.H.Oort
    (c) H.W.M. Olbers   (d) Ernst Opik

41. Who established the exact mechanism of the generation of energy inside the sun and other stars?
    (a) Meghnad Saha   (b) Geoffrey Burbidge
    (c) Hans Bethe   (d) Carl von Weizsackar

42. Who forwarded the now widely accepted theory that comets are dirty snowballs?
    (a) Fred Hoyle   (b) Frank L. Whipple
    (c) Giovanni Donati   (d) Wilhalm von Biela

43. Who developed the Aperture Synthesis technique for improving the resolution of radio objects?
    (a) J.S. Hey   (b) Martin Ryle
    (c) B.Y. Mills   (d) J.D. Kraus

44. Who prepared the New General Catalogue – NGC in short – of nebulae and clusters of stars?
    (a) J.L.E Dreyer   (b) Giovanni Cassini
    (c) Charles Messier   (d) John Herschel

45. Who forwarded the famous nebular hypothesis for the origin of the solar system?
    (a) Pierre Simon de Laplace
    (b) G.P. Kuiper
    (c) William de Sitter   (d) George Gamow

46. Who developed the Interferometry technique in radio astronomy to obtain sharper pictures of the radio universe?
    (a) B.Y. Mills   (b) Walter Baade
    (c) Robert Hanbury-Brown
    (d) Martin Ryle

47. Who devised the widely used knife-edge test for checking the figure of the mirror?
    (a) Leon Foucault   (b) Christiaan Huygens
    (c) Robert Hooke   (d) James Nasmyth

48. Who developed the technique for measuring the distance of distant stars?
    (a) Edward Pickering   (b) Christian Doppler
    (c) Friedrich W. Bessel   (d) Henrietta S. Leavitt

49. Who determined the velocity of light by an astronomical method – timing the eclipses of Jupiter's moons by the planet?
    (a) Galileo Galilei   (b) James Bradley
    (c) E.W. Morley   (c) Olaus Roemer

Discoverers

50. Who discovered Neptune?
    - (a) J.G. Galle
    - (b) J.C. Adams
    - (c) Urbain Leverrer
    - (d) Clyde Tombaugh

51. Who discovered solar flares?
    - (a) William Herschel
    - (b) Richard C. Carrington
    - (c) Donald Menzel
    - (d) Edward Sabine

52. Who discovered gaps in the asteroid belt, where no asteroids are present?
    - (a) Giovanni Cassini
    - (b) Charles Kowal
    - (c) Giuseppe Piazzi
    - (d) Daniel Kirkwood

53. Who discovered the milli-second pulsar?
    - (a) Shrinivas Kulkarni
    - (b) Jocelyn Bell
    - (c) J.S. Hey
    - (d) Martin Ryle

54. Who discovered the Trojan satellites, a group of asteroids that are in the orbit of Jupiter around the sun?
    - (a) G.P. Kuiper
    - (b) William Lassell
    - (c) Wilhelm Beer
    - (d) Maximilian Wolf

55. Who discovered the element Helium in the sun, long before it was found on earth?
    - (a) Norman Lockyer
    - (b) Pierre Jenssen
    - (c) Gustav Kirchhoff
    - (d) Willam Ramsey

56. Who discovered a type of galaxy with a very bright nucleus?
    (a) Harlow Shapley   (b) Carl Seyfert
    (c) Robert J. Trumpler   (d) Walter Baade

57. Who discovered the asteroid Ceres?
    (a) J.E. Bode   (b) Caroline Herschel
    (c) Giuseppe Piazzi   (d) Anonymous

58. Who discovered Cosmic rays?
    (a) Bruno B. Rossi   (b) Victor F. Hess
    (c) Robert A. Millikan   (d) Frederick Reines

59. Who discovered Chiron, a peculiar member of the solar system?
    (a) J. Hedley Robinson   (b) Charles Kowal
    (c) J. E. Bode   (d) John Herschel

60. Who discovered the star-like, yet extremely bright, objects called 'quasars'?
    (a) Maarten Schmidt
    (b) Jesse Leonard Greenstein
    (c) Allan Sandage   (d) Herbert Friedman

61. Who discovered the moons of Mars?
    (a) Tycho Brahe   (b) Asaph Hall
    (c) E.M. Antoniadi   (d) Mikhail Lomonosov

62. Who discovered the aberration of starlight – the apparent displacement in the position of a star as a result of the earth's movement around the sun?
    (a) David Gregory   (b) James Bradley
    (c) Jean Pons   (d) Giuseppe Piazzi

Inventors

63. Who invented the reflecting telescope?
    (a) William Herschel   (b) William Parsons
    (c) Isaac Newton   (d) Galileo Galilei

64. Who invented the achromatic lens that corrected chromatic aberration in images?
    (a) W.H. Wollaston   (b) Joseph von Fraunhofer
    (c) Josef von Utzschneider
    (d) John Dollond

65. Who invented the Gregorian telescope?
    (a) David Gregory   (b) James Gregory
    (c) Pope Gregory XIII (d) None

66. Who invented the Spectroheliograph designed to photograph the sun in the light of one particular wavelength?
    (a) John Evershed   (b) George Ellery Hale
    (c) Pietro Secchi   (d) Warren de la Rue

67. Who invented the infrared telescope?
    (a) Gerry Neugebauer   (b) Frank Low
    (c) James Dewar   (d) David Allen

68. Who invented the Bolometer and made a careful
    measurement of solar radiation?
    (a) Samuel P. Langley   (b) William Crookes
    (c) Joseph W. Swan   (d) William Thomson

69. Who invented the Coronograph that allowed the study
    of the sun without waiting for a total solar eclipse?
    (a) John Evershed   (b) Bernard Lyot
    (c) Pierre Jenssen   (d) Donald Menzel

70. Who invented the Transit instrument used to mark
    the passage of stars across the meridian?
    (a) Olaus Roemer   (b) John Dolland
    (c) William Bond   (d) Jesse Ramsden

71. Who invented the Schmidt telescope or camera that
    can photograph relatively wide areas of the sky with
    one exposure?
    (a) Julius Schmidt   (b) Berhard Schmidt
    (c) Both   (d) None

III

PORTRAIT QUIZ

72. Who is this 'visible' British astronomer and astrophysicist?
    - (a) Fred Hoyle
    - (b) Hermann Bondi
    - (c) Martin Ryle
    - (d) Stephen W. Hawking

73. Who is this smiling Indian radio astronomer?
    - (a) V. Balasubramanian
    - (b) V.R Venugopal
    - (c) Ch. V. Sastry
    - (d) Govind Swarup

74. Who is this medieval astronomer known to every student of astronomy?
    - (a) Johann Kepler
    - (b) Tycho Brahe
    - (c) Galileo Galilei
    - (d) Nicolaus Copernicus

75. Who is this Indian–born astrophysicist and a Nobel Laureate?
    (a) Shrinivas Kulkarni
    (b) Shiv Kumar
    (c) S.K. Kundu
    (d) S. Chandrasekar

76. Who is this British astronomer well-known for the discovery of an astronomical phenomenon on Indian soil?
    (a) Donald C. Mitchie
    (b) Norman Lockyer
    (c) John Evershed
    (d) N.R. Pogson

77. Who is this eminent Indian astronomer, the first to become the President of the International Astronomical Union?
    (a) J.C. Bhattacharya
    (b) K.D. Abhyankar
    (c) M.K.V. Bappu
    (d) S.M. Aladdin

78. Who is this famous astronomer known more on account of a heavenly body?
    (a) Edmund Halley
    (b) Bart J. Bok
    (c) J.H. Oort
    (d) Galileo Galilei

79. Who is this early modern astronomer?
   - (a) James Bradley
   - (b) William Herschel
   - (c) Johannes Hevelius
   - (d) John Herschel

80. Who is this most talked about astrophysicist?
   - (a) Lyman Spitzer Jr.
   - (b) Arthur S. Eddington
   - (c) Carl Sagan
   - (d) Stephen W. Hawking

81. Who is this world famous Indian astrophysicist, the son of a village grocer?
   - (a) Jayant V. Narlikar
   - (b) S. Chandrasekher
   - (c) Meghnad Saha
   - (d) S.M Alladin

IV

OBSERVATORIES AND INSTRUMENTS

Observatories

82. Who founded the first real observatory in Europe with the patronage of a king?
    - (a) Galileo Galilei
    - (b) Isaac Newton
    - (c) Tycho Brahe
    - (d) Nicolaus Copernicus

83. Which observatory has the largest refractor in the world today ?
    - (a) Lick Observatory
    - (b) Siding Spring Observatory
    - (c) Yerkes Observatory
    - (d) European Southern Observatory

84. Who built a huge astronomical observatory in Samarkand, now in Uzbekisthan?
    - (a) Al-kashi
    - (b) Ulugh Beg
    - (c) Alhazen
    - (d) Omar Khayyam

85. Who built a chain of five observatories of masonry structures in medieval India?
    (a) Sawai Jai Singh II   (b) Jahangir
    (c) Bhaskaracharya   (d) Pandit Jagannath

86. A flying astronomical observatory is named after an eminent astronomer. Who is he?
    (a) Bernard Lovell   (b) George Ellery Hale
    (c) Otto Struve   (d) G.P Kuiper

87. Where is the Lick Observatory with the world's second largest refractor located?
    (a) Mount Wilson   (b) Mount Palmer
    (c) Mount Hamilton   (d) Tucson

88. Which Russian Observatory was completely destroyed during World War II and has been rebuilt since?
    (a) Crimean Astronomical Observatory
    (b) Sterberg Institute Observatory
    (c) Mountain Observatory of Academy of Sciences
    (d) Pulkovo Astronomical Observatory

89. What is the ideal place for an astronomical observatory?
    (a) Space   (b) Mountain top
    (c) Lakeside   (d) Seashore

90. Who founded the famous Royal Greenwich Observatory?
    (a) John Flamsteed   (b) Edmund Halley
    (c) William Herschel   (d) King Charles II

91. A satellite observatory launched some time ago was named in honour of an Indian-born astrophysicist. Who is he?
    (a) S. Chandrasekhar   (b) Shiv K. Kumar
    (c) Shrinivas Kulkarni   (d) M.K.V. Bappu

92. Which space observatory is likely to throw more light on extra-solar planets?
    (a) Chandra X-ray Observatory
    (b) Space Infrared Telescope Facility
    (c) Hubble Space Telescope
    (d) Mars Express Orbiter

93. Which observatory has been able to detect the presence of neutrinos coming from the sun?
    (a) Brookhaven National Observatory
    (b) Sudbury Neutrino Observatory
    (c) Booster Neutrino Experiment
    (d) Russian-American Gallium Solar Neutrino Experiment

Telescopes

94. What is a telescope with a convex objective and a concave eyepiece known as?
    (a) Newtonian telescope
    (b) Cassegrain telescope
    (c) Hubble telescope   (d) Galilean telescope

95. Which type of telescope is favoured by amateur astronomers because it is easy to use?
    (a) Cassegrain telescope (b) Gregorian telescope
    (c) Maksutov telescope (d) Newtonian telescope

96. Which radio telescope is installed in a natural bowl-shaped valley?
    (a) Jodrell Bank Radio Telescope
    (b) Arecibo Radio Telescope
    (c) Ooty Radio Telescope
    (d) Very Large Array Telescope

97. Which nineteenth century astronomer was fond of building huge reflecting telescopes?
    (a) Johnnes Hevelius   (b) Warren de la Rue
    (c) George Airy   (d) Lord Rosse

98. Where is the Multiple Mirror Telescope located?
    (a) Mount Hopkins   (b) Mount Palmer
    (c) Mount Wilson   (d) Mount Hamilton

99. Which is the most commonly used reflecting telescope?
    (a) Newtonian telescope (b) Cassegrain telescope
    (c) Gregorian telescope (d) Schmidt telescope

100. What type of mounting do small telescopes generally have?
    (a) Altazimuth mounting   (b) German mounting
    (c) Yoke mounting   (d) Horseshoe mounting

101. In which mountain was a major telescope installed for the first time?
  - (a) Mount Palmer
  - (b) Mount Stromlo
  - (c) Mount Hamilton
  - (d) Mount Wilson

102. The Space Telescope presently orbiting the earth is named in honour of this astronomer. Who is he?
  - (a) Edwin P. Hubble
  - (b) Harlow Shapley
  - (c) Otto Struve
  - (d) Bernard Lowell

Instruments and Devices

103. Which instrument is used to determine the presence of elements and molecules in celestial objects?
  - (a) Spectrometer
  - (b) Radiometer
  - (c) Spectrograph
  - (d) Spectroscope

104. Which device increases the brightness of an image or the intensity of an electrical signal?
  - (a) Charged Coupled Device
  - (b) Photovoltaic Cell
  - (c) Photometer
  - (d) Photomultiplier

105. Which instrument is used to determine the diameters of stars or galaxies?
  - (a) Interferometer
  - (b) Photometer
  - (c) Radiometer
  - (d) Spectrometer

106. Which is the essential component of a telescope meant to study the sun?
    (a) Siderostat
    (b) Coelostat
    (c) Heliostat
    (d) Heliometer

107. What produces electronic images in a modern telescope?
    (a) Charge-Coupled Device
    (b) Grating
    (c) Coude
    (d) Achromatic lens

108. Which device demonstrates the motion of the planets and the Moon in the solar system?
    (a) Planetarium
    (b) Siderostat
    (c) Orrery
    (d) No such device exists

109. Which instrument is used to study the corona of the sun through a telescope?
    (a) Magnetograph
    (b) Collimator
    (c) Coronograph
    (d) Sextant

110. Which instrument is used to detect differences in two photographs taken of the same region of the sky?
    (a) Spectrometer
    (b) Sextant
    (c) Blink Microscope
    (d) Speckle Interferometer

111. Which instrument is used for conducting astronomical photography?
    (a) Spectrograph
    (b) Astrograph
    (c) Photometer
    (d) Quadrant

V

SKY WATCHER PHOTO QUIZ

112. Which is this huge American optical telescope?
     (a) Hale Telescope
     (b) Hooker Telescope
     (c) Mcmath Telescope
     (d) Du Pont Telescope

113. These huge radio dishes aimed at the sky are part of
     a European Observatory. Which is it?
     (a) Mullard Radio Astronomy
         Observatory
     (b) Max Planck Institute for
         Radio Astronomy
     (c) Nuffield Radio Astronomy
         Laboratory
     (d) Westerbork Radio
         Observatory

114. It is the second largest optical telescope in the world. Which observatory has this telescope?
    (a) Cerro Tololo Inter-American Observatory
    (b) Siding Spring Observatory
    (c) Crimean Astrophysical Observatory
    (d) Hale Observatory

115. It is the world's largest solar telescope. Which observatory has this telescope?
    (a) McDonald Observatory
    (b) European Southern Observatory
    (c) Northern Hemisphere Observatory
    (d) Kitt Peak National Observatory

116. This Y-Shaped radio telescope is the largest in the world today. What is it called?
    (a) Ryle Telescope
    (b) Very Large Array
    (c) Mark I
    (d) Reber Telescope

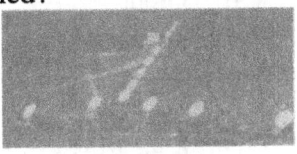

117. This is the original site of a world famous observatory today. Which is that observatory?
    (a) Royal Greenwich Observatory
    (b) Olaus Roemer Observatory
    (c) Griffith Observatory
    (d) Lowell Observatory

118. Which Indian observatory has this telescope?
    (a) U.P State Observatory
    (b) Vainu Bappu Observatory
    (c) Kodaikanal Observatory
    (d) Japal-Rangapur Observatory

119. Which Indian science body has this radio telescope?
    (a) Indian Institute of Astrophysics
    (b) Indian Institute of Science
    (c) National Center for Radio
        Astrophysics
    (d) Raman Research Institute

120. This is one of the five astronomical observatories
    built in medieval India. Where is this particular
    observatory located?
    (a) New Delhi
    (b) Jaipur
    (c) Varanasi
    (d) Ujjain

121. This is an artist's impression of the first modern
    astronomical observatory built on Indian soil.
    Where was it located?
    (a) Mumbai
    (b) Chennai
    (c) Kolkata
    (d) Cochin

VI

PRINCIPLES AND UNITS

Principles and Practices

122. Which effect is used for determining the velocities of celestial objects?
     - (a) Raman effect
     - (b) Doppler effect
     - (c) Wilson-Bappu effect
     - (d) Wilson effect

123. 'Oh, Be A Fine Girl, Kiss Me Right Now!' This unforgettable mnemonic is meant to remember the classification of objects. Which ones?
     - (a) Galaxies
     - (b) Stars
     - (c) Nebulae
     - (d) Pulsars

124. The inertial properties of a piece of matter are in some way attributable to the influence of all other matter in the universe. What is this statement called?
     - (a) Mach's principle
     - (b) Anthromorphic principle
     - (c) Cosmological principle
     - (d) Heisenberg principle

125. Which law in astronomy has yet no scientific justification?
    (a) Kepler's law   (b) Newton's law
    (c) Bode's law   (d) Hubble's law

126. Which law states that the recession velocity of a distant extragalactic object is directly proportional to its distance?
    (a) Stefan's law   (b) Kepler's law
    (c) Sporer's law   (d) Hubble's law

127. How many parameters uniquely specify the position and the path of a celestial body in its orbit?
    (a) Six   (b) Three
    (c) Two   (d) Eight

128. The existence of life on earth determines the structure of the universe. What is this notion called?
    (a) Chandrasekhar's limit
    (b) Anthromorphic principle
    (c) Tippler's law   (d) No such notion exists

129. Which effect is used to determine the intensity of a star's magnetic field?
    (a) Compton effect   (b) Zeeman effect
    (c) Bappu-Wilson effect   (d) Raman effect

130. When a star is approaching us, the spectral lines of starlight shift towards this colour of the spectrum. Which one?
   (a) Red
   (b) Orange
   (c) Blue
   (d) Yellow

131. When three celestial bodies come in a straight line, what is it called?
   (a) Synergy
   (b) Resonance
   (c) Syzygy
   (d) Eclipse

Units and Measurements

132. The unit of strength of a radio wave emission is named in the honour of a radio astronomer. Who is he?
   (a) J.S. Hey
   (b) Grote Reber
   (c) Karl Jansky
   (d) R.H. Dicke

133. Which type of motion of a star is measured by the shift in its spectral lines?
   (a) Proper motion
   (b) Radial motion
   (c) True motion
   (d) All

134. Which unit of length is used for measuring the distances within the solar system?
   (a) Light year
   (b) Parsec
   (c) Kilometre
   (d) Astronomical Unit

135. What is the measure of the true brightness of a star?
   (a) Absolute magnitude
   (b) Apparent magnitude
   (c) Visual magnitude   (d) Luminosity

136. What unit of angular measure is used for measuring angles that celestial objects or their separation subtend at the observer?
   (a) Arc   (b) Arc second
   (c) Parsec   (d) All

137. What is the measure of the extent to which an elliptical orbit departs from circularity?
   (a) Ellipsis   (b) Eclipsis
   (c) Eccentricity   (d) Anomaly

138. Which unit of length is often used to measure interstellar distances?
   (a) Astronomical Unit   (b) Parsec
   (c) Lightyear   (d) All

139. What is the measure of relative brightness of stars and other celestial objects?
   (a) Luminosity   (b) Apparent magnitude
   (c) Magnitude   (d) Visual magnitude

140. An 'Astronomical Unit' is the mean distance between the sun and one of the following planets. Which is it?
     (a) Pluto   (b) Mercury
     (c) Earth   (d) Mars

141. What is a celestial latitude equivalent to?
     (a) Azimuth   (b) Right Ascension
     (c) Declination   (d) All

VII

HEAVENLY BODIES AND THE UNIVERSE

Small Bodies

142. Which Jupiter's satellite has a smooth ice-covered surface crossed by fracture lines?
     - (a) Io
     - (b) Ganymede
     - (c) Elara
     - (d) Europa

143. Most of the asteroids are in a belt lying between the orbits of two planets. Which ones?
     - (a) Saturn and Jupiter
     - (b) Jupiter and Mars
     - (c) Mars and Venus
     - (d) Uranus and Neptune

144. Which minor body is an earth-grazer?
     - (a) Atan
     - (b) Hermes
     - (c) Icarus
     - (d) All

145. Which planet has the highest number of moons discovered so far?
    (a) Jupiter
    (b) Satuen
    (c) Uranes
    (d) Pluto

146. Which type of meteorite is stony-iron?
    (a) Aerolites
    (b) Chondrites
    (c) Siderolite
    (d) Siderite

147. Which moon of Saturn is partly very dark and partly very bright?
    (a) Iapetus
    (b) Hyperion
    (c) Phoebe
    (d) Dione

148. Which asteroid comes closest to the earth?
    (a) Ceres
    (b) Pallas
    (c) Eros
    (d) Hebe

149. What are 'Shepherd moons' concerned with?
    (a) Periodic comet
    (b) Plantesimal size
    (c) Meteor shower
    (d) Ring system

150. Which is the moon of Mars?
    (a) Deimos
    (b) Iapetus
    (c) Triton
    (d) None

151. Where is the 'Kuiper belt' located in the solar system?
    (a) Between orbits of Mars and Jupiter
    (b) Around the orbit of Saturn
    (c) Between orbits of Saturn and Uranus
    (d) Around the orbit of Pluto

152. Which heavenly bodies are nowadays believed to have brought water – and even pre-biotic life – to the surface of the earth?
    (a) Apollo objects   (b) Comets
    (c) Asteroids   (d) Meteors

153. Which heavenly body has been named in honour of the Indian-born American astronaut Kalpana Chawla?
    (a) Apollo object   (b) Kuiper object
    (c) Comet   (d) Asteroid

154. Where is located the heavenly body 'Varuna' named after an Indian deity?
    (a) Near Mercury   (b) In an orbit of Moon
    (c) Beyond Neptune   (d) In an orbit of Jupiter

155. Which comet crashed into Jupiter creating a spectacular astronomical event in 1994?
    (a) Comet Hyakutake
    (b) Comet Shoemaker-Levy
    (c) Comet Hale-Bobb   (d) Comet Halley

156. What is the estimated minimum size of a heavenly body, which can wipe out most, if not all, human beings on the earth?
    (a) 33-44 kilometres   (b) 11-22 kilometres
    (c) 44-55 kilometres   (d) 22-33 kilometres

157. Where are Apollo-Amor objects found?
    (a) Between Jupiter and Saturn
    (b) Inside the orbit of the earth
    (c) Between Venus and Mars
    (d) Beyond Pluto

158. What is believed to be the source of origin of tektites– small, glassy, round objects found only in certain parts of the world?
    (a) Interstellar space   (b) Moon
    (c) Asteroids   (d) Mercury

The Moon

159. What does the Moon lack?
    (a) Atmosphere   (b) Central core
    (c) Magnetic field   (d) Crust

160. When is 'Harvest Moon' – the full Moon – seen?
    (a) March equinox   (b) June solstice
    (c) December solstice   (d) September equinox

161. What is the source of origin of the Moon?
    (a) Earth   (b) Minor bodies
    (c) Nebula that created the solar system
    (d) Nothing is clear as yet

162. Which is the largest *mare* region on the Moon?
    (a) *Mare Lmbrium*   (b) *Mare Serenitatis*
    (c) *Mare Fecunditatis*   (d) *Oceanus Procellarum*

163. What is the age of the Moon?
    (a) 4600 million years   (b) 3600 million years
    (c) 5600 million years   (d) 2600 million years

164. What causes erosion on the surface of the Moon?
    (a) Wind   (b) Lava
    (c) Micrometeorites   (d) No erosion occurs

Planets

165. Of the following outer planets, which is the odd one out?
    (a) Pluto   (b) Earth
    (c) Saturn   (d) Neptune

166. Which gas in the Venusian atmosphere is mainly responsible for the existence of very high temperatures on its surface?
    (a) Methane   (b) Nitrogen
    (c) Ammonia   (d) Carbon dioxide

167. Which planet's ring was discovered by the *Voyager-I* spacecraft?
    (a) Jupiter   (b) Saturn
    (c) Uranus   (d) Neptune

168. Which planet does not have thunderstorms in its atmosphere?
    (a) Mars   (b) Venus
    (c) Jupiter   (d) Saturn

169. Which planet has the largest moon in the solar system?
    (a) Saturn   (b) Jupiter
    (c) Mars   (d) Earth

170. Which gaseous planet has two satellites?
    (a) Neptune   (b) Mars
    (c) Jupiter   (d) Uranus

171. What are planets supposed to be made of?
    (a) Planetesimals   (b) Planetoids
    (c) Minor planets   (d) Meteorites

172. Which planet takes 88 days to go around the sun once ?
    (a) Mercury   (b) Saturn
    (c) Venus   (d) Uranus

173. To which planet was the *Cassini* spacecraft sent for its study?
    (a) Pluto   (b) Jupiter
    (c) Saturn   (d) Uranus

174. To which planet was the *Galileo* spaceprobe sent for its study?
    (a) Saturn   (b) Jupiter
    (c) Neptune   (d) Uranus

175. Which planet has a natural structure on its surface resembling a human face, leading to considerable speculation on its discovery?
    (a) Mercury   (b) Mars
    (c) Venus   (d) Jupiter

176. Which planet is likely to be colonized in the near future?
    (a) Venus   (b) Mercury
    (c) Mars   (d) Jupiter

177. Which is the only planet having a relative density less than that of water?
    (a) Neptune   (b) Uranus
    (c) Saturn   (d) Jupiter

178. Which is the planet that comes closest to the earth in its orbit?
    (a) Mercury   (b) Jupiter
    (c) Mars   (d) Venus

179. Which planet has the Great Red Spot on its sur face?
    (a) Saturn   (b) Pluto
    (c) Jupiter   (d) Neptune

The Sun

180. How much time does the sun takes to rotate once about its axis?
    (a) About 24 hours   (b) About 11 hours
    (c) About 11 days   (d) About 24 days

181. Which spectral class does the sun belong to?
    (a) G   (b) F
    (c) O   (d) K

182. What is the mean density of the sun?
    (a) 1.4   (b) 2.5
    (c) 6.9   (d) 10.4

183. Which part of a sun's atmosphere appears red to the naked eye during a total solar eclipse?
    (a) Photosphere   (b) Corona
    (c) Chromosphere   (d) None

184. What type of star is our sun?
   - (a) Red giant
   - (b) Yellow dwarf
   - (c) White dwarf
   - (d) Supergiant

185. What is the visible round face of the sun technically known as?
   - (a) Photosphere
   - (b) Chromosphere
   - (c) Corona
   - (d) Heliosphere

186. What kind of matter is a solar wind?
   - (a) Gaseous
   - (b) Plasmic
   - (c) Solid
   - (d) Liquid

187. Where does the phenomenon called 'Space storm' occur?
   - (a) Solar corona
   - (b) Solar photosphere
   - (c) Solar chromosphere
   - (d) All

188. Which part of the sun's atmosphere extends many millions of kilometres into space?
   - (a) Corona
   - (b) Photosphere
   - (c) Chromosphere
   - (d) Granule

189. Which star is similar to our sun?
   - (a) Beta Orionis
   - (b) Alpha Scorpii
   - (c) Epsilon Eridani
   - (d) Tau Ceti

Stars

190. Which is presently the northern pole star?
    (a) Zeta Ursae Majoris
    (b) Xi Ursae Majoris
    (c) Gamma Ursae Minoris
    (d) Alpha Ursae Minoris

191. Which famous star is a red supergiant?
    (a) Antares
    (d) Deneb
    (c) Castor
    (d) Vega

192. Which star is a recurrent nova?
    (a) T. Coronae Borealis (b) R. Hydrae
    (c) Beta Lyrae
    (d) Kappa Pavonis

193. Which famous star actually consists of six stars?
    (a) Rigel
    (b) Castor
    (c) Fomalhaut
    (d) Aldebaran

194. Which is the southern pole star?
    (a) Sigma Octantis
    (b) Lambda Octantis
    (c) Tau Octantis
    (d) None

195. Which is a pulsating star?
    (a) Theta Tauri
    (b) Arcturus
    (c) R.R. Lyrae
    (d) Acrux

196. Which is a flare star?
    (a) Delta Cephei   (b) W. Ursae Majoris
    (c) UV Ceti   (d) R. Coronae Borealis

197. Where have stars been found to collide with each other more frequently?
    (a) Globular cluster   (b) Nebula
    (c) Oort cloud   (d) Asteroid belt

198. Which nuclear reaction provides energy to keep the star shining?
    (a) Hydrogen conversion into helium
    (b) Carbon conversion into nitrogen
    (c) Nitrogen conversion into lead
    (d) Helium conversion into carbon

199. Which is a giant star?
    (a) Arcturus   (b) Epsilon Aurigae
    (c) P. Cygni   (d) Polaris

200. Whether a star has a planet or not is inferred from this. What is it?
    (a) Luminosity   (b) Temperature
    (c) Motion   (d) Companions

201. Which is the star closest to the sun?
    (a) Beta Centauri   (b) Proxima Centauri
    (c) 3 Centauri   (d) Alpha Centauri

Galaxies

202. Which one of the following types of bright galaxies is in the majority?
    - (a) Spiral
    - (b) Elliptical
    - (c) Lenticular
    - (d) Irregular

203. Which is a satellite galaxy of our own?
    - (a) Andromeda
    - (b) Small Magellanic Cloud
    - (c) NGC 185
    - (d) Large Magellanic Cloud

204. What type of structure does our galaxy have?
    - (a) Elliptical
    - (b) Lenticular
    - (c) Spiral
    - (d) Irregular

205. Where does most of the interstellar gas and dust in our galaxy lie?
    - (a) Galactic plane
    - (b) Spiral arms
    - (c) Central halo
    - (d) Everywhere

206. Which is the first radio galaxy to be identified?
    - (a) 3C 236
    - (b) Sagittarius A
    - (c) NGC 5128
    - (d) Cygnus A

207. Where are the Magellanic Clouds, two neighbourly small galaxies, located?
   (a) Carina
   (b) Dorado
   (c) Pictor
   (d) Puppis

208. How many major types of galaxies are there?
   (a) Three
   (b) Four
   (c) Two
   (d) Five

209. Which galaxy contains the sun?
   (a) NGC 205
   (b) Milky Way
   (c) Andromeda
   (d) Centaurus A

210. Which galaxy is visible to the naked eye?
   (a) Whirlpool
   (b) Black Eye
   (c) M74
   (d) Andromeda

211. Who noticed the spiral structure in galaxies?
   (a) Load Rosse
   (b) John Herschel
   (c) William Herschel
   (d) Stephen Alexander

Celestial Objects

212. Which is the most powerful radio source in the sky?
   (a) Cassiopeia A
   (b) Cassiopeia B
   (c) Cygnus A
   (d) Centaurus A

213. What could be the possible source for the enormous energy output of a quasar?
    (a) White hole
    (b) Neutron star
    (c) Black hole
    (d) White dwarf

214. Which heavenly body undergoes the quiescent phase regularly?
    (a) Moon
    (b) Jupiter
    (c) Sun
    (d) Mars

215. Which heavenly body moves in a parabolic orbit?
    (a) Planet
    (b) Sun
    (c) Natural satellite
    (d) Comet

216. Which is considered to represent the best observational evidence for the existence of a black hole?
    (a) Cygnus A
    (b) Cygnus X-1
    (c) Centaurus A
    (d) Cassiopeia A

217. Which is a globular cluster?
    (a) Messier 42
    (b) Omega Centauri
    (c) 3C 273
    (d) Sagittarius A

218. A Local Group is a small cluster of this. What is it?
    (a) Stars
    (b) Galaxies
    (c) Nebulae
    (d) Minor planets

219. Which heavenly body does librations, allowing us to see at least 60 per cent of its otherwise 'fixed' face towards us?
    (a) Mercury   (b) Moon
    (c) Sun   (d) Mars

220. Where does 'degenerate' matter occur?
    (a) Quasar   (b) White dwarf
    (c) BL. Lacertae object (d) Neutron star

221. When a collapsing object's radius shrinks to its Schwarzschild radius, what does it become?
    (a) White hole   (b) Neutron star
    (c) Black hole   (d) White dwarf

222. What kind of heavenly bodies emit synchrotron radiation?
    (a) Radio sources   (b) Supernova remnants
    (c) Newborn stars   (d) All

The Universe

223. Which theory of the origin of the universe do most astronomers favour?
    (a) Steady State theory   (b) Big Bang theory
    (c) Oscillating Universe theory
    (d) Big Crunch theory

224. What accounts for 99 per cent of the universe?
    (a) Solid   (b) Plasma
    (c) Liquid   (d) Gas

225. What is the main property of the background microwave radiation that favours the Big Bang model of the universe?
    (a) Isotropic   (b) Homogeneous
    (c) Non-Isotropic   (d) Chaotic

226. The universe must look the same at a given time to an observer located anywhere within the universe. What is this notion known as?
    (a) Perfect cosmological principle
    (b) Olber's paradox
    (c) Russell's paradox
    (d) Cosmological principle

227. What is the estimated age of the universe?
    (a) 20-30 billion years   (b) 5-10 billion years
    (c) 10-20 billion years   (d) 30-40 billion years

228. Which is the most abundant element in the universe ?
    (a) Helium   (b) Carbon
    (c) Lead   (d) Hydrogen

229. Who said, 'The greatest riddle of cosmology may well be ....that the universe is, in a sense, creative'?
   (a) Karl Popper
   (b) Roger Penrose
   (c) Stephen W. Hawking
   (d) John Wheeler

230. Which scientific idea is nowadays gaining ground in cosmology?
   (a) Open Universe   (b) Parallel Universes
   (c) Oscillating Universe   (d) All

231. Who discovered the faint microwave background radiation which lends support to the Big Bang theory of the origin of the universe?
   (a) Thomas Gold   (b) Arno Penzia
   (c) Hermann Bondi   (d) Robert Wilson

232. What are hypothesised to be the remnants of the early universe?
   (a) Proto-galaxies   (b) Quasars
   (c) Cosmic strings   (d) Gravitational lenses

233. There is only one eminent astrophysicist who still firmly believes in the 'Steady State Theory' of the universe. Who is he?
   (a) Fred Hoyle   (b) Hermann Bondi
   (c) J. V. Narlikar   (d) Stephen W. Hawking

VIII

OBSERVATIONAL

General

234. How many stars form the famous Orion belt?
    - (a) Seven
    - (b) Nine
    - (c) Three
    - (d) Five

235. What is the symbol used for the third brightest star in a constellation?
    - (a) Omega
    - (b) Alpha
    - (c) Beta
    - (d) Gamma

236. Which is the phase of the Moon after the New Moon, when its surface is half illuminated?
    - (a) Last quarter
    - (b) Waxing crescent
    - (c) Waning crescent
    - (d) First quarter

237. The 'Summer triangle' is made up of three bright stars which are seen during summer in the northern hemisphere. Which are those stars?
   (a) Spica, Alphard, and Arcturus
   (b) Regulus, Spica and Arcturus
   (c) Deneb, Vega, and Altair
   (d) Regal, Betelgeuse, and Aldebaran

238. Which is not the best time to observe the Moon?
   (a) Full Moon   (b) Gibbous Moon
   (c) First quarter   (d) Last quarter

239. Into how many regions is the entire sky divided?
   (a) 90   (b) 120
   (c) 88   (d) 64

240. When does the brilliant meteor shower called 'Leonids' occur in a year?
   (a) Around April 19th   (b) Around January 1st
   (c) Around November 15th
   (d) Around July 15th

241. What is the width of the zodiac belt?
   (a) About 20 degree
   (b) About 16 degree
   (c) About 10 degree   (d) About 8 degree

242. Which stars are called 'pointers'?
   (a) Alpha and Gamma Ursae Minoris
   (b) Nu and Psi Draconis
   (c) Alpha and Beta Ursae Majoris
   (d) Delta and Xi Cephei

243. Where is the 'Trapezium' consisting of four brightest stars located?
   (a) Orion   (b) Taurus
   (c) Gemini   (d) Eridanus

244. On are average how many comets are discovered every year?
   (a) Two   (b) Three
   (c) Four   (d) Six

Constellations

245. Which constellation is called the 'Great Dog'?
   (a) Canis Major   (b) Canes Venatici
   (c) Cepheus   (d) Cetus

246. Where is the famous open star-cluster Hyades located?
   (a) Auriga   (b) Canis Major
   (c) Gemini   (d) Taurus

247. Which is the most well-known southern constellation?
    (a) Crux   (b) Dorado
    (c) Corona Australis (d) Indus

248. Which constellation contains the present pole star, Polaris?
    (a) Ursa Minor   (b) Ursa Major
    (c) Cepheus   (d) Camelopardalis

249. How many constellations lie on the zodiac belt?
    (a) 16   (b) 20
    (c) 24   (d) 12

250. Which constellation is split into two separate halves?
    (a) Serpens   (b) Perseus
    (c) Cetus   (d) Carina

251. Which constellation is distinctly W-shaped?
    (a) Norma   (b) Lyra
    (c) Centaurus   (d) Cassiopeia

252. Which constellation contains the brightest globular cluster in the northern skies?
    (a) Andromeda   (b) Corona Borealis
    (c) Bootes   (d) Hercules

253. Which constellation does not belong to the zodiac belt?

(a) Lyra (b) Taurus

(c) Virgo (d) Pisces

254. Which constellation contains the showpiece 'Jewel Box', an open cluster of a variety of different-coloured stars?

(a) Tucana (b) Crux

(c) Carina (d) Lepus

255. Which constellation contains Messier 31, one of the most famous object in the entire sky?

(a) Hercules (b) Andromeda

(c) Vela (d) Cassiopeia

Nebulae

256. Where is the flower-like Rosette nebula located?

(a) Orion (b) Lepus

(c) Monoceros (b) Canis Minor

257. Where is the brilliant and colorful Triffid nebula located?

(a) Capricornus (b) Sagittarius

(c) Scorpius (d) Aquila

258. What is the Messier Object Number for Orion nebula?
   - (a) 1
   - (b) 42
   - (c) 8
   - (d) 17

259. Where is the attractive Dumb-bell nebula located?
   - (a) Hercules
   - (b) Aquila
   - (c) Vulpecula
   - (d) Lyra

260. Where is the famous planetary Ring nebula, which looks like a smoke ring, located?
   - (a) Draco
   - (b) Lyra
   - (c) Vulpecula
   - (d) Cygnus

261. Where is the Coalsack nebula located?
   - (a) Lyra
   - (b) Eridanus
   - (c) Carina
   - (d) Crux

262. Where is the spidery Tarantula nebula located?
   - (a) Pictor
   - (b) Carina
   - (c) Hydrus
   - (d) Dorado

Celestial Phenomena

263. Which body is associated with the phenomenon of faculae?
   - (a) Moon
   - (b) Mars
   - (c) Jupiter
   - (d) Sun

264. A total solar eclipse can never last for more than this duration. How long is it?
    (a) 12 min and 8 sec
    (b) 4 min and 50 sec
    (c) 2 min and 45 sec
    (d) 7 min and 40 sec

265. What phenomenon is the popular Great Red Spot?
    (a) Volcanic eruption
    (b) Cloud
    (c) Storm center
    (d) None of the above

266. Where is the 'Earthshine' seen?
    (a) Mercury
    (b) Moon
    (c) Venus
    (d) Mars

267. When are 'Baily's beads' seen?
    (a) Lunar eclipse
    (b) Solar eclipse
    (c) Magnetic storm
    (d) Solar flare

268. What is the phenomenon of 'Occultation' concerned with?
    (a) Solar wind
    (b) Eclipse
    (c) Magnetic storm
    (d) Corona

269. Where is believed to be the boundary of heliopause in which solar wind and magnetic field give way to dust particles and stellar magnetic fields?
    (a) Beyond Neptune
    (b) Beyond Pluto
    (c) Beyond Moon
    (d) Beyond Jupiter

270. At what speed does the Moon's shadow travel over the surface of the earth?
   (a) About 3,000 km per hour
   (b) About 3,000 m per hour
   (c) About 3,000 km per second
   (d) About 3,000 m per second

271. Which heavenly phenomenon is believed to affect food production on earth?
   (a) Supernova   (b) Occultation of a star
   (c) Sun spots   (d) Solar eclipse

IX

HEAVENLY PORTRAIT QUIZ

272. Which planet or its moon has this huge structure on its surface?
    (a) Ganymede
    (b) Venus
    (c) Titan
    (d) Mars

273. Which is this nebula?
    (a) Horseshoe nebula
    (b) Dumbbell nebula
    (c) Swan nebula
    (d) Horsehead nebula

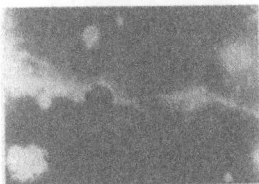

274. This is beautiful, easily seen, spiral galaxy Messier 81 Where is it located?
    (a) Centaurus
    (b) Dorado
    (c) Bootes
    (d) Ursa Major

275. Which nebula is this?
- (a) Veil nebula
- (b) Omega nebula
- (c) Lagoon nebula
- (d) Coalsack nebula

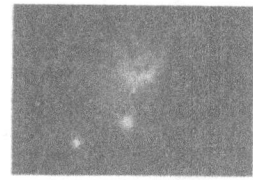

276. What is this heavenly body?
- (a) Star cluster
- (b) Planetary nebula
- (c) Globular cluster
- (d) Open cluster

277. Where is this famous Crab nebula located?
- (a) Sagittarius
- (b) Orion
- (c) Taurus
- (d) Gemini

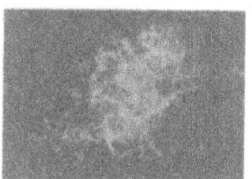

278. Which is this silvery moon?
- (a) Io
- (b) Callisto
- (c) Tethys
- (d) Ariel

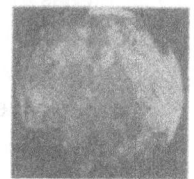

279. What is this object that fell in India called?
- (a) Meteorite
- (b) Tektite
- (c) Meteor
- (d) Meteoroid

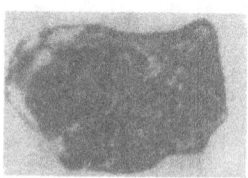

280. Which is this heavenly body?

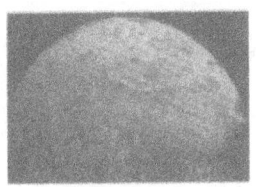

   (a) Europa
   (b) Triton
   (c) Oberon
   (d) Mercury

281. Which is this famous heavenly object?

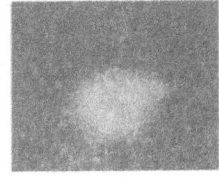

   (a) Venus
   (b) Halley's comet
   (c) The Jewel Box
   (d) Alpha Centauri

X

NICKNAMES, TERMS AND VALUES

Nicknames

282. What is the name of the hypothetical companion star to the sun?
    - (a) X-star
    - (b) Black hole
    - (c) Vulcan
    - (d) Nemesis

283. 'Hesperus' is the old name of one planet when it is visibleas evening star. Which one?
    - (a) Mercury
    - (b) Saturn
    - (c) Venus
    - (d) Jupiter

284. Which star cluster is more renowned as the 'Seven sisters'?
    - (a) Pleiades
    - (b) Messier 36
    - (c) Praesepe
    - (d) IC 2602

285. 'Little Dipper' is the American name of this constellation. Which one?
   (a) Canis Minor
   (b) Leo Minor
   (c) Ursa Minor
   (d) None of the above

286. What was called a 'Guest star' earlier?
   (a) Variable star
   (b) Eclipsing binary
   (c) Supernova
   (d) All

287. What was the name attributed to the planet once thought to be in orbit between Mercury and the sun?
   (a) Vulcan
   (b) Hesperus
   (c) Zeno
   (d) No name was given

288. Which star is known as the 'Winking Demon'?
   (a) Algol
   (b) Delta Cephei
   (c) Albireo
   (d) W. Ursae Majoris

289. A king nicknamed him 'Comet Ferret '. Who was he?
   (a) Edmund Halley
   (b) Giovanni Donati
   (c) Charles Messier
   (d) Johann Encke

290. Which planet is called 'Earth's twin'?
   (a) Mercury
   (b) Mars
   (c) Venus
   (d) Pluto

Terms

291. What is called a 'Superior planet'?
    (a) A gaseous planet
    (b) A planet beyond the orbit of the earth
    (c) A planet bigger than the earth
    (d) A planet more luminous than a star

292. What is the technical term for a 'Falling star'?
    (a) Meteor   (b) Meteorite
    (c) Supernova   (d) Comet

293. What are stars that are always above the horizon from the observer's latitude called?
    (a) Circumpolar stars   (b) Polar stars
    (c) Protostars   (d) Pointers

294. What is the moment called when a heavy object crosses the observer's meridian?
    (a) Opposition   (b) Culmination
    (c) Nadir   (d) Transit

295. What is the daily rotation of the heavens from East to West around the celestial poles called?
    (a) Diurnal motion   (b) Direct motion
    (c) Apparent motion   (d) Apsidal motion

296. When the surface of the Moon, Venus or Mercury is exactly half-lit, what is it called?
   (a) First quarter   (b) Dichotomy
   (c) Libration   (d) Halo

297. What is a brilliant, exploding meteor called?
   (a) Bolide   (b) Fireball
   (c) Ashen light   (d) Streaker

298. What does the term 'Planet' mean?
   (a) Wanderer   (b) Nomad
   (c) Bright object   (d) God-like being

299. 'Island universe' is an obsolete term for this. What is it?
   (a) Galaxy   (b) Nebula
   (c) Galactic cluster   (d) All

300. What is the creation of elements by nuclear reactions in stars known as?
   (a) Nucleonics   (b) Nuclear fusion
   (c) Nucleosynthesis   (d) Nuclear energy

Associations

301. What is the term 'Sidereal' associated with?
   (a) Planet   (b) Sun
   (c) Moon   (d) Star

302. What is the term 'Singularity' associated with?
- (a) Black hole
- (b) Neutron star
- (c) Red giant
- (d) Supernova

303. What is the term 'Figuring' associated with?
- (a) Lens
- (b) Mirror
- (c) Both the above
- (d) Filter

304. What is a 'Saros' associated with?
- (a) Solar eclipse
- (b) Sunspots
- (c) Lunar eclipse
- (d) Solar wind

305. What is the Hertzsprung-Russell diagram associated with?
- (a) Evolution of galaxies
- (b) Evolution of stars
- (c) Evolution of planets
- (d) All

306. What is the term 'Eccentricity' associated with?
- (a) Circular orbit
- (b) Perihelion
- (c) Elliptical orbit
- (d) Perigee

307. What is 'Window' associated with in astronomical jargon?
- (a) Wavelength
- (b) Transparency
- (c) Atmosphere
- (d) All

308. In astronomical parlance, the term 'Nucleus' is associated with this object. Which one?
   (a) Meteor
   (b) Asteroid
   (c) Planet
   (d) Comet

Subjects

309. Which branch of astronomy deals with the measurement of positions and motions of heavenly bodies?
   (a) Astrophysics
   (b) Astronomy
   (c) Astrology
   (d) Cosmology

310. Aerography is the study of the surface features of this body. Which one?
   (a) Moon
   (b) Mercury
   (c) Pluto
   (d) Mars

311. What is photographing the heavenly bodies known as?
   (a) Celestial photography
   (b) Astrophotography
   (c) Cosmo photography
   (d) Space photography

312. What is the study of the behaviour of electrically conducting fluids in magnetic fields, such as that of the sun, known as?
    (a) Hydrodynamics   (b) Geomagnetism
    (c) Magnetohydrodynamics
    (d) Magnetostatics

313. What is the study of the origin and evolution of the solar system known as?
    (a) Cosmogony   (b) Cosmology
    (c) Solar physics   (d) Planetary science

314. Which branch of astronomy deals with the motion of heavenly bodies?
    (a) Spherical astronomy (b) Special relativity
    (c) Astrodynamics   (d) Celestial mechanics

315. What is the study of the Moon's physical features called?
    (a) Lunar science   (b) Cartography
    (c) Selenology   (d) Selenography

316. What is the study of the physical and chemical processes and characteristics of celestial bodies and intervening space known as?
    (a) Cosmology   (b) Stellar physics
    (c) Astrophysics   (d) Cosmogony

Values

317. What is the value of the solar constant?
    (a) 136.7 kilowatts per square metre
    (b) 13.67 kilowatts per square metre
    (c) 0.1367 kilowatts per square metre
    (d) 1.376 kilowatts per square metre

318. How many days are in a sidereal month – the time taken for the Moon to go once around the earth?
    (a) About 27.55 days (b) About 29.53 days
    (c) About 27.32 days (d) About 31.28 days

319. What is the value of one lightyear?
    (a) 9.46×10^{12} km   (b) 9.46×10^{10} km
    (c) 9.46×10^{14} km   (d) 9.46×10^{8} km

320. What is taken as the longitude of Greenwich Meridian for all astronomical measurements?
    (a) 90 degree   (b) 0 degree
    (c) 180 degree   (d) 270 degree

321. What is the albedo of the Moon?
    (a) 0.7   (b) 0.0007
    (c) 0.007   (d) 0.07

322. Whose value has been altered drastically since its original formulation?
    (a) Astronomical Unit
    (b) Hubble constant
    (c) Solar radius
    (d) Gravitational constant

323. Who much is one Astronomical Unit?
    (a) 172, 679, 798 kilometres
    (b) 153, 290, 261 kilometres
    (c) 149, 597, 870 kilometres
    (d) 112, 472, 918 kilometres

324. What is the value of Hubble's constant?
    (a) 17 m/sec per million lightyears
    (b) 17 km/hour per million lightyears
    (c) 17 km/sec per billion lightyears
    (d) 17 km/sec per million lightyears

325. What is the mean density of Jupiter?
    (a) 2.7
    (b) 1.3
    (c) 0.7
    (d) 3.2

XI

THE PAST

Old Astronomy

326. Which people had once a special department of Government called 'Astronomical Bureau or Directorate' that kept watch on the heavens for any unusual development?
   (a) Mayas   (b) Indians
   (c) Chinese   (d) Greeks

327. What use was the knowledge of heavenly bodies first put to?
   (a) Determination of time (b) Navigational aid
   (c) Measuring the earth   (d) Building temples

328. Where did the concept of lunar mansions – the constellations or groups of stars in the path of the Moon in the sky – originate?
   (a) China   (b) India
   (c) Arabia   (d) All

329. Where in the medieval time was a chain of stations for the seasonal observations of the noon sun shadows covering a length of 2,500 km established?
(a) Peru
(b) Chain
(c) Easter Island
(d) Italy

330. Where were stonehenges built to keep track of the Moon and the sun?
(a) Britain
(b) France
(c) Canada
(d) Hawaii

331. Which ancient instrument is used for determining the altitude of a star?
(a) Quadrant
(b) Siderostat
(c) Sextant
(d) Meridian circle

332. Which ancient system of the universe contained the concept of deferents and epicycles?
(a) Copernican
(b) Aristotelian
(c) Ptolemaic
(d) Aristarchan

333. When the Great Pyramid of Giza was constructed, which star was the earth's pole star?
(a) Delta Cephei
(b) Psi Draconis
(c) Gamma Cassiopeiae
(d) Thuban

334. Which star provided an annual warning of the great floods of the Nile to the Egyptians?
    (a) Arcturus   (b) Sirius
    (c) Deneb   (d) Altair

Old Indian Astronomy

335. What are 'Rahu' and 'Ketu' associated with in ancient Indian astronomy?
    (a) Phases of the Moon (b) Eclipses
    (c) Comets   (d) Supernova

336. Which ancient Indian text was brought to Baghdad and translated into Arabic thus imparting ancient Hindu astronomical traditions to the Arab world?
    (a) *Siddhantasekhara* (b) *Siddhanta-darpana*
    (c) *Brahmasphuta-siddhanta*
    (d) *Vatesvara-siddhanta*

337. Who wrote *Siddhanta-Siromani*, the most comprehensive 'Siddhanta' work in Indian astronomy?
    (a) Nilakantha Somayaji (b) Bhaskara II
    (c) Sripati   (d) Jnanaraja

338. Where were astrolabs and celestial globes built in the sixteenth and seventeenth century India?
    (a) Bijapur   (b) Varanasi
    (c) Agra   (d) Lahore

339. Which Indian King built telescopes for use in his kingdom?
    (a) Shivaji
    (b) Sawai Jai Singh II
    (c) Surajmal
    (d) None

340. Which astronomical events are associated with 'tithi' the basis of several Hindu religious festivals?
    (a) Lunar eclipses
    (b) Solar eclipses
    (c) Solar cycles
    (d) Lunar phases

341. Which Moghul Emperor was the first to receive a telescope as a gift from a European?
    (a) Jahangir
    (b) Muhammad Shah
    (c) Akbar
    (d) Aurangzeb

342. What is called 'Rasi Chakra' in ancient Indian astronomical tradition?
    (a) Constellation
    (b) Zodiac belt
    (c) Instrument
    (d) Eclipse

343. What brought developments in astronomy in Europe to medieval India?
    (a) Churches
    (b) Arabic books
    (c) Jesuit missionaries
    (d) Sailors

344. How many types of astronomical works, Siddhantas, are there?
    (a) Three
    (b) Four
    (c) Five
    (d) Six

345. Who wrote *Siddhanta Darpana*, a classic treatise on the traditional Indian astronomy also containing his own life-long researches in astronomy?
    (a) Varahamihira
    (b) Samanta Chandra Sekhar
    (c) Jagannath Samrat
    (d) Aryabhata

346. Which Indian astronomer built the handy 'Mana Yantra' to determine the height of a mountain, among other things?
    (a) Sawai Jai Singh II
    (b) Samanta Chandra Sekhar
    (c) Bhaskaracharya   (d) Aryabhata

347. Which is the oldest astronomical text in India?
    (a) *Graha-laghava*   (b) *Vedanga Jyotisha*
    (c) *Surya Siddhanta*   (d) *Aryabhatia*

348. How long is a 'Mahayuga', the Great Epoch, which is the most fundamental element of Indian astronomy?
    (a) 4,320,000 years   (b) 4,320,000,000 years
    (c) 4,320 years   (d) 432 years

349. In ancient India, what was 'astronomy' known as?
    (a) Science of stars
    (b) Science of constellations
    (c) Science of the night sky
    (d) Science of skywatchers

XII

CALENDARS AND DATES

Time

350. What is the Muslim calendar based on?
    (a) Movement of the sun
    (b) Movement of the stars
    (c) Phases of the Moon
    (d) Movement of the Mars

351. When is the adjustment for 365 ¼-days-long solar year made?
    (a) February 28   (b) December 31
    (c) June 30   (d) October 31

352. How many days are there in a calendar year?
    (a) 365.256 days   (b) 365.243 days
    (c) 365.259 days   (d) 365.242 days

353. When does the vernal equinox – the time day and night are equal all over the world – occur every year?
   (a) March 21
   (b) About March 21
   (c) September 23
   (d) About September 23

354. Which type of calendar was introduced in India during the rule of the Moghul Emperor Akbar?
   (a) Tarikh Ilahi
   (b) Julian calendar
   (c) Hejira calendar
   (d) Gregorian calendar

355. Which astronomical instrument was used earlier for precise time-keeping?
   (a) Telescope
   (b) Transit circle
   (c) Sextant
   (d) Astrolabe

356. When does the summer solstice – the time when the hours of daylight are longest – occur every year?
   (a) About July 31
   (b) About July 15
   (c) About June 21
   (d) About June 31

357. When is the adjustment for a 'leap second' – one second – made to compensate for the gradual slowing down of the rotation of the earth?
   (a) January 1
   (b) June 30
   (c) March 31
   (d) December 31

358. What was the present calendar originally known as?
   (a) Julian calendar
   (b) Gregorian calendar
   (c) Lunar calendar
   (d) Jewish calendar

Turning Points

359. When did Meghnad Saha forward his famous Ionisation formula, linking temperature and degree of ionisation in the atmosphere of stars?
   (a) 1921
   (b) 1947
   (c) 1932
   (d) 1956

360. Which year's solar eclipse confirmed that the light from star is bent by the gravitational pull of the sun proving Albert Einstein's General Theory of Relativity?
   (a) 1916
   (b) 1919
   (c) 1921
   (d) 1922

361. When was the first accurate estimate of the size of our galaxy, the Milky Way, placing the sun near its outer edge, made?
   (a) 1968
   (b) 1958
   (c) 1938
   (d) 1918

362. Which year was declared the International Geophysical year when several nations joined hands to study the effects of solar activity on the earth?
   (a) 1952-1953
   (b) 1954-1955
   (c) 1956-1957
   (d) 1957-1958

363. When was the International Astronomical Union, the controlling body of world astronomy, founded?
    (a) 1957   (b) 1919
    (c) 1938   (d) 1952

364. When did Galileo Galilei discover the four moons of Jupiter – a sound evidence indicating that not all bodies circle the earth – supporting Copernicus' Heliocentric theory?
    (a) 1640   (b) 1636
    (c) 1610   (d) 1627

365. When were extraterrestrial radio waves detected leading to the foundation of radio astronomy?
    (a) 1942   (b) 1954
    (c) 1923   (d) 1931

366. When did a group of astronomers meet in Washington D.C., and decide that Greenwich is the prime meridian of the earth?
    (a) 1921   (b) 1896
    (c) 1912   (d) 1884

367. Uranus was the first 'modern' planet to be discovered in the night sky. When was that?
    (a) 1792   (b) 1776
    (c) 1781   (d) 1804

368. When was the well-known Royal Greenwich Observatory founded in England?
   (a) 1685   (b) 1675
   (c) 1695   (d) 1665

Important Dates

369. When did the mysterious Tunguska event – the falling of an outer space object on the earth – occur?
   (a) 1897   (b) 1906
   (c) 1920   (d) 1913

370. When was the Cosmic Background Explorer (COBE) launched into space to study remnant radiations of the early universe?
   (a) 1989   (b) 1999
   (c) 1969   (d) 1979

371. When was a *New General Catalogue of Nebulas and Clusters of Star*, often referred to as NGC, published?
   (a) 1888   (b) 1900
   (c) 1902   (d) 1904

372. When was the planet Pluto discovered?
   (a) 1940   (b) 1950
   (c) 1930   (d) 1920

373. The Roman Catholic Inquisition forced Galileo Galilei to give up the Copernican view that the earth moves around the sun. When was the Inquisition held?

(a) 1629   (b) 1633

(c) 1642   (d) 1638

374. When was the first modern *Nautical Almanac* published?

(a) 1834   (b) 1902

(c) 1856   (d) 1914

375. When was the reputed Royal Astronomical Society founded in England?

(a) 1860   (b) 1880

(c) 1890   (d) 1820

376. When was the first Kuiper belt object discovered ?

(a) 1972   (b) 1982

(c) 1992   (d) 2002

377. When was the first planet outside the solar system discovered?

(a) 2001   (b) 1981

(c) 1971   (d) 1991

378. What is considered to be the 'Golden Age of Theoretical Research in the Black Hole'?

(a) 1964-1975   (b) 1976-1984

(c) 1985-1990   (d) 1991-2003

XIII

LITERATURE AND QUOTES

Literature

379. Which among the following poets wrote treatises on astronomy?
    (a) Lord Byron (b) Geoffrey Chaucer
    (c) William Wordsworth (d) Robert Frost

380. Who calculated the date, when Vedic literature of the Hindus was written, on the basis of certain astronomical observations made in it?
    (a) B.G. Tilak (b) H. Jacob
    (c) John Bentley (d) All

381. Which novel of Thomas Hardy has an astronomical observatory as the meeting point of two lovers?
    (a) *Under the Greenwood Tree*
    (b) *Two on a Tower*
    (c) *The Trumpet-Major* (d) *Jude the Obscure*

382. In which literary work has the author explained how the creator intervened to account for the obliquity of the earth's axis?
    (a) *The Divine Comedy* (b) *Don Quixote*
    (c) *Paradise Lost*   (d) *Volpone*

383. Who wrote the poem *Astronomer's Drinking Song*?
    (a) Augustus de Morgan (b) Lord Byron
    (c) Geoffrey Chaucer   (d) J.J. Sylvester

384. Which classical writer said that for a proper understanding of poetry the knowledge of astronomy is essential?
    (a) Quintillian   (b) Pliny the Elder
    (c) Kalidasa   (d) Plato

385. Which astronomer is also considered to be the founder of Russian literature?
    (a) Aristarch Belopolsky
    (b) I. Shklovsky
    (c) G. Sholomitsky   (d) Mikhail Lomonosov

386. Which astronomical idea is the central theme of Isaac Asimov's famous story *Nightfall*?
    (a) Life on a blackhole.
    (b) Life in a multiple-star system.
    (c) Life on an asteroid.
    (d) Life on a planet circling a nova star.

387. Who wrote *Natural History*, which contains all the important assumptions and theories of classical astronomy?
  (a) Pliny the Elder   (b) Thales
  (c) Theophrastus   (d) Aristarchus

388. Who wrote *The Black Cloud* containing an encounter with a cloud-like intelligent alien?
  (a) Fred Hoyle   (b) Larry Niven
  (c) Robert L. Forward   (d) Johann Kepler

389. Who wrote the science fiction *Contact* involving time travel through an astronomical concept?
  (a) Isaac Asimov   (b) Arthur C. Clarke
  (c) Carl Sagan   (d) Fred Hoyle

Language

390. When somebody behaves erratically, his or her temperament is qualified by this heavenly object. Which one?
  (a) Pulsar   (b) Mercury
  (c) Nova   (d) Mars

391. Whenever anything is to be called common or base, this planet is often used as an adjective. Which one?
  (a) Saturn   (b) Venus
  (c) Mercury   (d) Earth

392. When somebody is to be called eccentric or deranged, this heavenly body is used as an adjective. Which one?
   (a) Moon
   (b) Meteor
   (c) Mercury
   (d) Comet

393. A proverb containing a heavenly object is mentioned when somebody is urged to take advantage of favourable circumstances. Which is that heavenly object?
   (a) Supernova
   (b) Sunspot
   (c) Sun
   (d) Galaxy

394. When somebody rises very fast in any field, he or she is considered to be following the footsteps of this heavenly body. Which one?
   (a) Supernova
   (b) Comet
   (c) Meteor
   (d) Nova

395. Which heavenly body has become associated with filmdom?
   (a) Star
   (b) Moon
   (c) Quasar
   (d) Black Hole

396. Which heavenly body is referred to when somebody's brilliant qualities are discussed?
   (a) Star
   (b) Jupiter
   (c) Sun
   (d) All

397. When somebody is urged not to hide one's talent, the proverb containing this astronomical instrument is mentioned. Which is the instrument?
    (a) Telescope   (b) Sextant
    (c) Sundial   (d) Spectroscope

398. Which heavenly body is often referred to when a beautiful face is described?
    (a) Sun   (b) Star
    (c) Venus   (d) Moon

399. When one is grateful to one's luck, it is attributed to the influence of this heavenly body. Which one?
    (a) Meteor   (b) Comet
    (c) Sun   (d) Star

Quotations

400. Which philosopher remarked, 'There is in the universe neither centre nor circumference'?
    (a) Giordano Bruno   (b) Aristotle
    (c) Regiomontanus   (d) Omar Khayyam

401. Who said, 'Reflectors very seldom do good work except in the hands of their makers'?
    (a) William Lassell (b) Howard Grubb
    (c) John Dolland   (d) James Nasmyth

402. Which astronomer said, 'The universe begins to look more like a great thought than like a great machine'?
   (a) Percival Lowell   (b) Harlow Shapley
   (c) Nicolaus Copernicus (d) James Jeans

403. Which comet hunter often said, 'One cannot discover comets lying in bed'?
   (a) Charles Messier   (b) William R. Brooks
   (c) Lewis Swift   (d) William von Biela

404. Who said, 'The universe is full of magical things patiently waiting for our wits to grow sharper'?
   (a) R.W. Emerson   (b) Eden Phillpotts
   (c) J.B.S. Haldane   (d) Albert Einstein

405. Which writer remarked, 'May be this world is another planet's hell'?
   (a) Aldous Huxley   (b) C.S. Lewis
   (c) George Orwell   (d) Albert Camus

406. Who remarked, 'The effort to understand the universe is one of the very few things that lifts human life a little above the level of farce and gives it some of the grace of a tragedy'?
   (a) George Gamow   (b) Steven Weinberg
   (c) William de Sitter   (d) Thomas Gold

407. Who said, 'Any sufficiently advanced Extraterrestrial Intelligence is indistinguishable from God'?
   (a) Arthur C. Clarke   (b) Michael Shermer
   (c) Carl Sagan   (d) Govind Swarup

408. Who said, 'For all we know, our own universe may have started in some one's basement'?
   (a) Hermann Bondi   (b) Alan Guth
   (c) Max Lerner   (d) Woody Allen

409. Who said, 'Astronomy is like the Ministry. No one should go into it without a "call"'?
   (a) M. K. V. Bappu   (b) Edwin P. Hubble
   (c) Fred Hoyle   (d) Otto Struve

410. Who quipped, 'What fun it would be to spend life doing cosmology at the taxpayer's expense'?
   (a) Woody Allen   (b) Ieuan Maddock
   (c) Groucho Marx   (d) Anonymous

411. Which astronomer remarked, 'When an electron vibrates, the universe shakes'?
   (a) Albert Einstein   (b) Fred Hoyle
   (c) Arthur S. Eddington   (d) Robert Wilson

XIV

CULTURE AND MYTHS

Culture

412. Which heavenly body is believed to forebode evil
     events, such as, plague, political upheavals, earth
     quakes, etc, on the earth?
     (a) Supernova   (b) Saturn
     (c) Comet   (d) Asteroid

413. During which Hindu festival is the Moon not
     supposed to be seen?
     (a) *Ganesh Chaturthi* (b) *Diwali*
     (c) *Holi*   (d) *Janamashtami*

414. Where in the ancient world was a solar eclipse
     believed to be caused by a dragon and all one could
     do to save the sun was to scare the dragon away by
     beating drums, shouting and screaming?
     (a) India   (b) Greece
     (c) Peru   (d) China

415. During the *Ramdan* month food is eaten by the Muslims during the absence of this heavenly body. Which is it?
    (a) Moon
    (b) Mercury
    (c) Sun
    (d) Venus

416. During which astronomical phenomenon are Hindu pregnant woman not allowed to do any work?
    (a) Lunar eclipse
    (b) Occultation of a star
    (c) Supernova occurrence
    (d) Solar eclipse

417. Which celestial phenomenon is often an occasion for a religious pilgrimage and holy bath?
    (a) Occultation of a star
    (b) Appearance of sunspots
    (c) Appearance of a comet
    (d) Solar eclipse

418. Evil spirits are believed to become active during this phase of the Moon. Which is it?
    (a) Gibbous Moon
    (b) Full Moon
    (c) New Moon
    (d) Half-Moon

419. The sighting of this beautiful phenomenon is believed to forebode an evil turn of events to the observer. What is it?
    (a) Supernova explosion
    (b) Nova explosion
    (c) Sunspots
    (d) Meteor flash

420. During a Hindu festival sweetened milk is partaken only after its shown to the Full Moon. Which festival?
   (a) *Ramnavmi*
   (b) *Kojagiri purnima*
   (c) *Janamashtami*
   (d) *Dussehra*

421. Which planet is often referred to as an evil influence?
   (a) Saturn
   (b) Mercury
   (c) Mars
   (d) Venus

Myths and Symbols

422. Which constellation is known as 'Saptarshi' or Seven Wise Men in Indian mythology?
   (a) Bootes
   (b) Leo
   (c) Ursa Major
   (d) Orion

423. Which religious place has a stony meteorite at the place of worship?
   (a) Varanasi
   (b) Jerusalem
   (c) Haridwar
   (d) Mecca

424. According to ancient Indian tradition, there are two Ganga rivers, one in the country and the other in the sky – *Akash Ganga*. What is it?
   (a) Our galaxy
   (b) Globular cluster
   (c) Pleiades
   (d) Zodiac belt

425. Which epic poem contains astronomy blended with characters and events?
   (a) *Ramayana*   (b) *Gilgamesh*
   (c) *Iliad*   (d) *Mahabharata*

426. Which heavenly body is the maternal uncle of all in Hindu folk tales, legends and mythology?
   (a) Mars   (b) Moon
   (c) Sun   (d) Comet

427. Which nation's flag is called 'the stars and stripes'?
   (a) United States (b) Canada
   (c) New Zealand   (d) Senegal

428. Which civilisation had the legend of the God Quetsalcoatl, consisting basically of astronomical details about the planet Venus?
   (a) The Babylonian (b) The Sumerian
   (c) The Aztec   (d) The Greek

429. Which nation's flag has a crescent Moon and a star?
   (a) Ghana   (b) Pakistan
   (c) Turkey   (d) Saudi Arabia

430. Which hero of the epic *Mahabharata* knew the art of predicting a solar eclipse?
   (a) Krishna   (b) Arjun
   (c) Jayadratha   (d) Abhimanyu

XV

RECORDS AND CURIOSITIES

Records

431. Which is the largest and brightest globular cluster in the sky?
    (a) 47 Tucanae
    (b) Omega Centuri
    (c) Messier 15
    (d) Messier 13

432. Which is the largest moon in the solar system?
    (a) Titan
    (b) Callisto
    (c) Ganymede
    (d) Triton

433. Which is the largest asteroid?
    (a) Eros
    (b) Pallas
    (c) Vesta
    (d) Ceres

434. Which planet has the least eccentric orbit around the sun?
    (a) Venus
    (b) Mercury
    (c) Mars
    (d) Earth

435. Where is the world's largest fully steerable radio telescope located?
    (a) Jodrell Bank, England   (b) Kodaikanal, India
    (c) Bonn, Germany   (d) Arecibo, Puerto Rico

436. Which is the most massive star known to date?
    (a) Eta Carinae   (b) HD 38268
    (c) Betelgeuse   (d) Plaskett's star

437. Which planet rotates the fastest about its axis?
    (a) Saturn   (b) Jupiter
    (c) Mars   (d) Mercury

438. Which is the fastest moving star in the sky?
    (a) Pollux   (b) Spica
    (c) Castor   (d) Barnard's star

Curiosities

439. Which reputed astronomer had discovered a satellite of Venus?
    (a) William Herschel   (b) Giovanni Cassini
    (c) E.E. Barnard   (d) Asaph Hall

440. Which planet had a striking feature that was observed by reputed astronomers till the last century but is missing now?
    (a) Mercury   (b) Venus
    (c) Mars   (d) Pluto

441. Who laid claim for a second moon in orbit around the earth at the turn of the century on the basis of his astronomical observation?
    (a) W. Spill
    (b) Philipp Fauth
    (c) Godfrey Sykes
    (d) G. Waltemath

442. Which heavenly bodies were once called the 'Vermin of the skies'?
    (a) Asteroids
    (b) Comets
    (c) Meteors
    (d) Meteoroids

443. Who played the role of a villain in not allowing J.C. Adams to pursue his interests so that he could not discover Neptune?
    (a) Johann Galle
    (b) George Airy
    (c) Warren de la Rue
    (d) John Herschel

444. What was at one time referred to as the 'Hole in the havens'?
    (a) Orion nebula
    (b) Rosette nebula
    (c) Rho Ophiuchi nebula
    (d) Crab nebula

445. Which heavenly bodies are believed to be tunnels to other universes?
    (a) Black holes
    (b) Cosmic strings
    (c) Quasars
    (d) No such body exists

446. Which reputed astronomer claimed that the sun was like any other planet with a glowing atmosphere and inhabitants?
   (a) William Herschel   (b) John Flamsteed
   (c) J.E Bode   (d) All

447. Which celestial object was jokingly referred to as the 'Little Green Men'?
   (a) Cepheid variable   (b) Quasar
   (c) Barnard's star   (d) Pulsar

Extraterrestrial Life

448. What does the space surrounding the sun or any star, which is conducive to the existence of life, called?
   (a) Exosphere   (b) Biosphere
   (c) Endosphere   (d) Ecosphere

449. Who forwarded the idea of drawing huge geometrical symbols, such as crops planted in regular patterns, on the earth so that inhabitants of other planets could see them and try to communicate with us?
   (a) Carl F. Gauss
   (b) Joseph Louis Lagrange
   (c) Mikhail Lomonosov
   (d) Nicolas Flammarion

450. Which search for extraterrestrial intelligence uses internet-connected computers all over the world?
    (a) SETI @ home   (b) Project Ozma
    (c) Project Phoenix   (d) NASA SETI Project

451. All the observatories of the world which conduct searches for extraterrestrial life now have this signia. What is it?
    (a) Flag of the Earth   (b) Emblem of the Earth
    (c) Sovenir of the Moon (d) Earth Medal

452. Where is the Search for Extraterrestrial Intelligence Institute located?
    (a) Cambridge, UK   (b) California, USA
    (c) Sydney, Australia   (d) Lyons, France

453. What is the study of alien life forms called?
    (a) ETology   (b) Alienolgy
    (c) Xenology   (d) Exobiology

454. Who said, 'Man is not alone in the universe, any more than the individual is alone in the group, or any one society alone among other societies'?
    (a) Margaret Mead   (b) Claude Levi-Strauss
    (c) Thor Heyerdahl   (d) Lewis Mumford

455. Which heavenly body is presently the most attractive target for the search for extraterrestrial life?
   (a) Titan   (b) Miranda
   (c) Europa   (d) Phobos

456. Who stated the law of parsimony: 'In no case may we interpret an action as the outcome of the exercise of a higher mental faculty if it can be interpreted as the exercise of one that stands lower on the psychological scale',which is commonly used in the search for extraterrestrial life?
   (a) Arthur C. Clarke   (b) Lloyd Morgan
   (c) Frank Drake   (d) Ben Bova

457. What would the 'Dyson Spheres' – signs of an advanced extraterrestrial civilisation – emit into the surrounding space, announcing their presence?
   (a) Ultraviolet rays   (b) X-rays
   (c) Infrared rays   (d) Nuclear radiations

458. Which astronomer proposed the need for developing standards for sterilisation of spacecrafts sent to other planets so that they don't get cont-aminated with terrestrial microbes?
   (a) Carl Sagan   (b) Fred Hoyle
   (c) Chandra Wickramasinghe
   (d) Sidney Coleman

459. Where was the Project Ozma that searched for extraterrestrial intelligence on radio waves initiated?
    (a) Jodrell Bank
    (b) Green Bank
    (c) Arecibo
    (d) Westerbork

460. Who first gave the idea of searching for alien civilisations through radio waves?
    (a) Carl Sagan
    (b) Frank Drake
    (c) Philip Morrison
    (d) Guiseppe Cocconi

461. Who sincerely believed in the presence of intelligent life on Mars on the basis of his own observations?
    (a) Percival Lowell
    (b) Giovanni Schiaparelli
    (c) Nicolas Flammarion
    (d) A.C.B. Lowell

462. Who forwarded the now famous equation giving the probability of finding extraterrestrial intelligence in the universe ?
    (a) Frank Drake
    (b) Freeman Dyson
    (c) Govind Swarup
    (d) Phillip Morrison

XVI

ASTRONOMY IN INDIA

Modern Indian Scene

463. Where is the Balloon Facility of the Tata Institute of Fundamental Research for conducting various astronomical studies located?
    (a) Ahmedabad   (b) Hyderabad
    (c) Bangalore   (d) Mumbai

464. Where is the second oldest Nizamiah Observatory in the country located?
    (a) Agra   (b) Salem
    (c) Patna   (d) Hyderabad

465. Who was the first in India to watch the sky using an optical telescope and make astronomical discoveries?
    (a) Jeremiah Shakerley   (b) Father J. Tieffenthaler
    (c) J.F. Tennant   (d) Father J. Richaud

466. Where is the biggest solar telescope in the country located?
   (a) Udaipur   (b) Kodaikanal
   (c) Naini Tal   (d) Leh

467. Where is the Gamma ray Telescope in the country located?
   (a) Leh   (b) Gulmarg
   (c) Kodaikanal   (d) Kavalur

468. Where is the Lonar crater located?
   (a) Maharashtra   (b) Madhya Pradesh
   (c) Uttar Pradesh   (d) Orissa

469. Where is the Positional Astronomy Centre that publishes astronomical almanacs and provides other astronomy-related services regularly located?
   (a) Kolkata   (b) Kharagpur
   (c) Shillong   (d) Varanasi

470. Which astronomical effect was discovered in the country?
   (a) Bappu-Wilson Effect (b) Evershed Effect
   (c) Wilson Effect   (d) Razin Effect

471. Where is the Gurushikhar Infrared Observatory located?
   (a) Javadi Hills   (b) Mount Nimmu
   (c) Mount Abu   (d) Dehra Dun

472. The minor planet 2596 is named in honour of an Indian astronomer. Who is he?
    (a) J.C Bhattacharaya   (b) M.K.V Bappu
    (c) Govind Swarup   (d) K.D Abhyankar

473. Where is the Giant Meter-wave Radio Telescope (GMRT) operating at meter radio waves installed in the country?
    (a) Near Jorhat   (b) Near Pune
    (c) Near Haridwar   (d) Near Ujjain

474. Where is the Inter University Centre for Astronomy and Astrophysics for training manpower and conducting researches for various astronomical studies located?
    (a) Shillong   (b) Pune
    (c) Bangalore   (d) Bhubaneswar

475. Where is the National Centre for Radio Astrophysics for conducting radio astronomical studies located?
    (a) Udaipur   (b) Jorhat
    (c) Pune   (d) Hyderabad

476. Where is the Decametre-wave Radio Telescope located in the country?
    (a) Ladakh   (b) Belasore
    (c) Gauribidanur   (d) Tripura

477. Who conducted pioneering studies on cosmic rays even using home-made balloons in the country?
    (a) Meghnad Saha   (b) D. S. Kothari
    (c) Govind Swarup   (d) Homi J. Bhabha

478. Which Indian radio relescope is also partcipating in the search for extraterrestrial signals?
    (a) Ooty Radio Telescope
    (b) Giant Meter-wave Radio Telescope
    (c) Decameter-wave Radio Telescope
    (d) All

479. Which Indian astronomer discovered an asteroid for the first time?
    (a) R. Rajamohan   (b) M. K. V. Bappu
    (c) J. C. Bhattacharya   (d) N. C. Rana

480. Where was the first planetarium in the country established?
    (a) Pune   (b) Guwahati
    (c) Kolkata   (d) Jaipur

481. Where was radio telescope installed for the first time in the country?
    (a) Udhagamandalam   (b) Dehra Dun
    (c) Kalyan   (d) Hassan

482. Which heavenly body is the target of the Indian space mission in 2008 ?
    (a) Moon
    (b) Ceres
    (c) Mercury
    (d) Phobos

483. Which Indian astronomer predicted the presence of Pluto in 1911 much before other western astronomers did?
    (a) H.P. Bhatta
    (b) A.K Das
    (c) V.B Ketkar
    (d) A.L Narayan

XVII

SOCIETIES AND AWARDS

Societies

484. Which society brings out the annual *The Observer's Handbook*, a useful reference book for astronomical data and events of the forthcoming year?
    (a) Royal Astronomical Society
    (b) Royal Astronomical Society of Canada
    (c) Royal Astronomical Society of the Pacific
    (d) British Astronomical Association

485. Which scientific body instituted a Prize of a large amount in 1900 to be awarded to the first person for communicating with the inhabitants of another planet?
    (a) British Astronomical Association
    (b) Paris Academy of Science
    (c) Royal Astronomical Society
    (d) Royal Bohemian Academy of Sciences

486. Where is the Astronomical Society of India located?
   (a) Bangalore (b) Chennai
   (c) Udaipur (d) Hyderabad

487. Which reputed society publishes monthly notices concerning astronomy?
   (a) American Astronomical Society
   (b) British Astronomical Association
   (c) Amateur Astronomer Association
   (d) Royal Astronomical Society

488. Where is the American Astronomical Society located?
   (a) Los Angeles (b) Chicago
   (c) Washington (d) New York

489. Where is the Royal Astronomical Society located?
   (a) Leicester (b) Oxford
   (c) London (d) Peterborough

Awards

490. Which body gives the Amateur Astronomer Medal to an individual for outstanding contributions to astronomy?
   (a) Amateur Astronomer Association
   (b) US National Academy of Sciences
   (c) American Astronomical Society
   (d) Astronomical League

491. Which Indian body gives the Vainu Bappu Memorial Award to an astrophysicist or astronomer for outstanding work in the subject?
    (a) Indian National Sciences Academy
    (b) National Academy of Science
    (c) Council of Scientific and Industrial Research
    (d) Indian Science Congress Association

492. Which body gives the Henry Draper Medal for outstanding research in astrophysics?
    (a) Amateur Astronomer Association
    (b) Royal Astronomical Society
    (c) US National Academy of Sciences
    (d) American Astronomical Society

493. Which body gives the Annie J. Cannon Award to a woman for outstanding contributions to astronomy?
    (a) US National Academy of Sciences
    (b) American Astronomical Society
    (c) American Institute of Physics
    (d) Society for Applied Spectroscopy

494. Which Indian body awards Amateur Astronomer Fellowships to enable amateur astronomers to spend some weeks in Indian astronomical institutions?
    (a) Astronomical Society of India
    (b) Indian Institute of Astrophysics
    (c) Indian National Science Academy
    (d) Indian Academy of Science

XVIII

BOOKS AND JOURNALS

Books

495. Who wrote the monumental *Historia Coelestis Britannica*?
    - (a) Edmund Halley
    - (b) John Flamsteed
    - (c) Isaac Newton
    - (d) James Bradley

496. Who wrote *Popular Astronomy*, which aptly followed its title to become the most popular nineteenth century book on astronomy?
    - (a) Nicolas Flammarion
    - (b) Hermann Vogel
    - (c) Davil Gill
    - (d) James Keeler

497. Which eminent astronomer wrote the thought-provoking *The Wisdom of Science*?
    - (a) Fred Hoyle
    - (b) Robert Hanbury-Brown
    - (c) Hermann Bondi
    - (d) M.K.V.Bappu

498. Who wrote *The Structure of the Universe* giving in details the origin of the universe and its present status, among other things?
    (a) Carl Sagan   (b) Jayant V. Narlikar
    (c) S. Chandrasekhar   (d) Robert Jastrow

499. Who wrote the monumental five-volume classic of the nineteenth century *Mecanique Celeste* (The Mechanisms of the Heavens) ?
    (a) William Herschel
    (b) Friedrich W. Bessel
    (c) Pierre-Simon Laplace
    (d) Carl F. Gauss

500. Who wrote the bestseller *The First Three Minutes* which gives in details the origin of the universe as the present science know it?
    (a) Carlos Rubbia   (b) Thomas Gold
    (c) Steven Weinberg   (d) Martin Rees

501. Who wrote the classic in astrophysics, *Introduction to the Study of Stellar Structure*, in which the evolution of white dwarf stars is explained?
    (a) Arthur S. Eddington
    (b) Martin Schwarzschild
    (c) Lyman Spitzer Jr.
    (d) S. Chandrasekhar

502. Who wrote the international bestseller *A Brief History of Time* which talks about the Big Bang theory and Black holes in extensive details?
    (a) Stephen W. Hawking (b) Antony Hewish
    (c) Hermann Bondi   (d) Jayant V. Narlikar

503. Who is the author of the ancient encyclopaedia of astronomy and mathematics, *The Almagest*?
    (a) Sosigenes   (b) Claudius Ptolemy
    (c) Hipparchus   (d) George von Peurbach

504. Who wrote *Astronomy in India*, an up to date account of astronomical developments in India?
    (a) Rajesh Kochhar   (b) T. Padmanabhan
    (c) Jayant V. Narlikar (d) S. Chandrasekhar

505. Who wrote the book *The Universe In A Nutshell*, an uptodate and masterful exposition of the subject in brief?
    (a) Stephen W. Hawking (b) Roger Penrose
    (c) Paul Davies   (d) Patrick Moore

506. Who wrote *Black Holes and Time Warps : Einstein's Outrageous Legacy*, a historical-cum-biograp-hical account of the most exotic objects in astro-physics?
    (a) Stephen W. Hawking (b) Kip S. Thorne
    (c) Fritz Zwicky   (d) John Wheeler

507. Who wrote the classic *Bharatiya Jyotish Sastra* on the history of astronomy in India?
    (a) K.S Shukla
    (b) S.N. Sen
    (c) S.B Dixit
    (d) K.V Sarma

508. Her ten volume catalogues of stars is her greatest contribution to astronomy. Who is she?
    (a) Anna Palmer Draper
    (b) Annie J. Cannon
    (c) Caroline Furness
    (d) Maria Mitchell

Journals and Other Things

509. Who edits the *Annual Yearbook of Astronomy*, which prints in addition to astronomical events of the year, some authoritative articles on the latest subjects and interesting experiences?
    (a) Simon Mitton
    (b) Heather Couper
    (c) Patrick Moore
    (d) Nigel Henbest

510. Who produced the first star atlas?
    (a) Tycho Brahe
    (b) Hipparchus
    (c) Regiomontanus
    (d) Alessandro Piccolomini

511. Who produced 'Selenographia', the first map of the Moon observable from the earth?
    (a) Johannes Hevelius
    (b) Christian Severin
    (c) Galileo Galilei
    (d) Not known

512. Which Indian science body publishes the *Journal of Astrophysics and Astronomy*?
    (a) Indian National Science Academy
    (b) National Academy of Sciences
    (c) Indian Academy of Sciences
    (d) Indian Astronomical Society

513. Who produced the first 'Photographic Map of the Entire Sky'?
    (a) E.C. Pickering   (b) L.M. Rutherfurd
    (c) George Rayet   (d) David Gill

XIX

MISCELLANY

514. Who discovered the 1987 A supernova in the Large Magellanic Cloud?
    - (a) Albert Jones
    - (b) Ian Shelton
    - (c) Rob McNaught
    - (d) All

515. Which subject has fired the imagination of astrophysicists in recent years and is now a subject of considerable research?
    - (a) Black Hole
    - (b) White Hole
    - (c) Big Bang
    - (d) Dark matter

516. Which astronomical effect came into news some time ago but became a controversy?
    - (a) Diamond-ring effect
    - (b) Jupiter effect
    - (c) Razin effect
    - (d) Wilson effect

517. What does the latest LIGO try to detect?
    - (a) Gravitational waves
    - (b) Cosmic Strings
    - (c) Black Holes
    - (d) Dark matter

518. Which dynasty of famous astronomers continued for four generations?
    (a) Struve   (b) Herschel
    (c) Lowell   (d) Schwarzschild

519. Which astronomer was an amateur boxing champion during his youth?
    (a) Allen Sandage   (b) Bernard Lowell
    (c) Edwin P. Hubble   (d) Peter van de Kamp

520. Which astronomer is more known for developing the technique of dating the past from rings of ancient trees?
    (a) Edward Maunder   (b) Donald Menzel
    (c) Heinrich Schwabe   (d) Andrew Douglass

521. Which eminent medieval astronomer was assassinated by his own son?
    (a) Ulugh Beg   (b) Claudius Ptolemy
    (c) Sawai Jai Singh II   (d) Alfonso X

522. Which eminent astronomer has become more famous for the temperature scales he devised rather than his contributions to astronomy?
    (a) Christian Mayer   (b) Mikhail Lomonosov
    (c) Carl F.Gauss   (d) Anders Celsius

523. Who used a comet as a symbol of melancholy in his famous engraving 'Melancholia'?
   (a) Albrecht Durer
   (b) Francesco de Volterra
   (c) Jan van Eyck
   (d) Andrea Mantegna

524. Which heavenly body is often mistaken for a flying saucer?
   (a) Orion Nebula
   (b) Mercury
   (c) Crab Nebula
   (d) Venus

525. Where is the biggest, well preserved meteor crater on the surface of the earth located?
   (a) Hoba, Africa
   (b) Lonar, India
   (c) Limerick, Ireland
   (d) Arizona ,USA

526. Where have 'Mascons' – regions of exceptionally high density – been found?
   (a) Moon
   (b) Io
   (c) Phobos
   (d) Titan

527. Where is the Oort cloud located?
   (a) Between Mercury and Sun
   (b) In the asteroid belt
   (c) Between Jupiter and Saturn
   (d) Beyond Pluto

528. Which is the heaviest molecule so far discovered in space?
    (a) Acetaldehyde   (b) Dimethyl ether
    (c) Ethanol   (d) Cyano-octatetrayne

529. Who said, 'Extraterrestrial life is an idea whose time has come'?
    (a) Frank Drake   (b) Phillip Morrison
    (c) Cael Sagan   (d) Freeman Dyson

530. Which of the following discoveries is still under a cloud of controversy?
    (a) Brown Dwarfs   (b) Free-floating planets
    (c) Millisecond pulsars (d) Red Giants

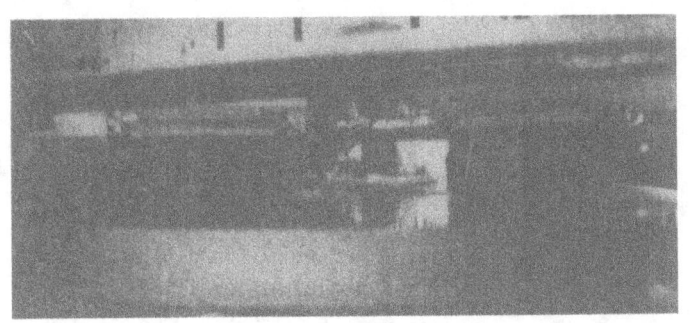

Q. 531 What is this huge round thing? What is this done on it? What is it meant for?

Q. 532 What is this beautiful instrument? What is its purpose?

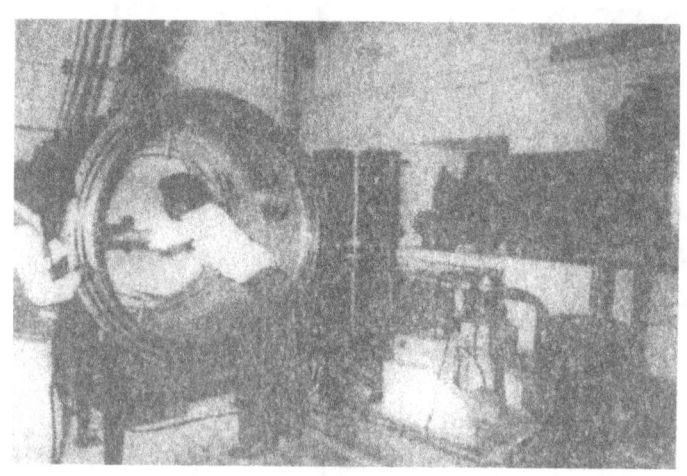

Q. 533 What is this chamber and other equipment?
What are their purposes?

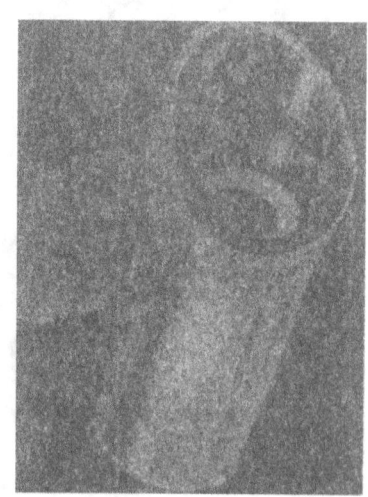

Q. 534 What is this
container-like thing?
What did it study?

Q. 535 Which is this instrument? What is it meant for?

Q. 536 What are these sky-watching dishes?
What is their purpose?

ANSWERS

1.(d)

2.(d)

3.(b) Known as 'Fraunhofer lines'

4.(c)

5.(c)

6.(a)

7.(b)

8.(c)

9.(d)

10.(a)

11.(a) and (b)

12.(b)

13.(a)

14.(b)

15.(b)

16.(a)

17.(c)

18.(c)

19.(a) Unknown to ancient people.

20.(a)

21.(d)

22.(d)

23.(b)

24.(a)

25.(c)

26.(c)

27.(a) Called 'Roche's limit'.

28.(c)

29.(b) and (d) each independently.

30.(b)

31.(a)

32.(c)

33.(c)

34.(a) and (d)

35.(d)

36.(c) Called 'Antoniadi scale' used by amateur astronomers.

37.(b) Called 'Metonic cycle'.

38.(d)

39.(a) Called 'Titius-Bode law'.

40.(c)

41.(c) and (d)

42.(b)

43.(b)

44.(a)

45.(a)

46.(c)

47.(a)

48.(d)

49.(d)

50.(a)

51.(b)

52.(d) Called 'Kirkwood gaps'.

53.(a)

54.(d)

55.(a)

56.(b) Called 'Seyfert galaxy'.

57.(c)

58.(b)

59.(b)

60.(a)

61.(b)

62.(b)

63.(c)

64.(d)

65.(b)

66.(b)

67.(b)

68.(a)

69.(b)

70.(a)

71.(b)

72.(a)

73.(d)

74.(a)

75.(d)

76.(c) Discovered 'Evershed effect' at Kodaikanal Observatory.

77.(c)

78.(a)

79.(b)

80.(d)
81.(c)
82.(c)
83.(c)
84.(b)
85.(a)
86.(d) Kuiper Airborne Observatory fitted aboard a transport plane.
87.(c)
88.(d)
89.(a)
90.(d)
91.(a) Chandra X-ray Observatory.
92.(b)
93.(b)
94.(d)
95.(d)
96.(b)
97.(d) Original name William Parsons.
98.(a)
99.(b)
100.(a)
101.(c)
102.(a)
103.(a)
104.(d)
105.(a)
106.(c)
107.(a)
108.(c)

109.(c)
110.(c)
111.(b)
112.(b)
113.(a)
114.(d)
115.(d)
116.(b)
117.(a)
118.(d) Near Hyderabad.
119.(c)
120.(b)
121.(b) Called 'Madras Observatory', it was set up by the East India Company.
122.(b)
123.(b)
124.(a)
125.(c) An empirical relationship essentially.
126.(d)
127.(a)
128.(b)
129.(b)
130.(c)
131.(c)
132.(c)
133.(b)
134.(d)
135.(a) and (d)

136.(b)
137.(c)
138.(b)
139.(c)
140.(c)
141.(c)
142.(d)
143.(b)
144.(d)
145.(a)
146.(c)
147.(a)
148.(c)
149.(d) Small moons keep ring particles in place.
150.(a)
151.(d)
152.(b)
153.(d)
154.(c)
155.(b)
156.(a)
157.(b)
158.(b) When Moon was volcanically alive, it threw some matter into space which reached the earth.
159.(a) and (c)
160.(d)
161.(d)

162.(d)
163.(a)
164.(c)
165.(b)
166.(d) Produces Greenhouse effect.
167.(a)
168.(a) Mars has dust storms.
169.(b)
170.(a)
171.(a)
172.(a)
173.(c)
174.(b)
175.(b)
176.(c)
177.(c)
178.(d)
179.(c)
180.(d)
181.(a) Exactly G2V spectral type.
182.(a)
183.(c)
184.(b)
185.(a)
186.(b)
187.(a) Called 'Coronal Mass Ejection' in technical parlance.
188.(a)
189.(c) and (d)

190.(d) Called 'Polaris'.
191.(a)
192.(a) Called 'Blaze star'.
193.(b)
194.(d) Sigma Octantis is nearest the pole.
195.(c)
196.(c)
197.(a)
198.(a) and (b)
199.(a)
200.(c)
201.(b) Alpha Centauri is the nearest star system, of which Proxima Centauri is the nearest to the sun.
202.(a)
203.(b) and (d)
204.(c)
205.(a)
206.(d)
207.(b)
208.(a)
209.(b) Sun on one of its spiral arms.
210.(d)
211.(a)
212.(a)
213.(c)

214.(c)
215.(d)
216.(b)
217.(b)
218.(b) Contains 25 galaxies.
219.(b)
220.(b) and (d)
221.(c)
222.(a) and (b)
223.(b)
224.(b)
225.(a)
226.(d)
227.(c) In accordance with the widely accepted Big Bang theory.
228.(d)
229.(a)
230.(b)
231.(b) and (d)
232.(c)
233.(c)
234.(c)
235.(d)
236.(d)
237.(c)
238.(a)
239.(c) Called 'Constellations'.
240.(c) Occurs in Leo constellation.
241.(b)

242.(c) They point at the pole star.
243.(a)
244.(d) An average rate.
245.(a)
246.(d)
247.(a) Contains pointers to the southern celestial pole.
248.(a)
249.(d)
250.(a)
251.(d)
252.(d)
253.(a)
254.(b) Southern Cross.
255.(b)
256.(c)
257.(b)
258.(b)
259.(c)
260.(b)
261.(d)
262.(d)
263.(d) Bright regions that appear before sunspots.
264.(d)
265.(c)
266.(b) Sunlight reflected by the earth on to the Moon.
267.(b) Especially total solar eclipse.
268.(b)
269.(b)
270.(a)
271.(c)
272.(d) Olympus Mons
273.(d)
274.(d)
275.(c)
276.(c)
277.(c)
278.(a)
279.(a) Muzaffarpur meteorite, 13.5 x 7.6 centimetres, fell on 10 April 1964.
280.(b)
281.(b) Much before it developed the tail.
282.(d)
283.(c)
284.(a)
285.(c)
286.(c)
287.(a)
288.(a)
289.(c)
290.(c)
291.(b)
292.(a)
293.(a)
294.(b)
295.(a)
296.(b)
297.(a)
298.(a)
299.(a)
300.(c)
301.(d)
302.(a)
303.(c) Grinding and polishing.
304.(a) and (b)
305.(b)
306.(c)
307.(d)
308.(d)
309.(b) Also called 'Positional Astronomy'.
310.(d)
311.(b)
312.(c)
313.(a)
314.(d)
315.(d)
316.(c)
317.(d)
318.(c)
319.(a)
320.(b)
321.(d)
322.(b)
323.(c)

324.(d)

325.(b)

326.(c)

327.(a)

328.(d) Controversial issue.

329.(b)

330.(a)

331.(a) Meridian circle is its modern version.

332.(c)

333.(d) Called 'Alpha Draconis'.

334.(b)

335.(b) 'Rahu' devoured the Moon or the sun and released it through its 'Ketu' tail.

336.(c)

337.(b)

338.(d)

339.(b)

340.(d) In ancient times, but in due course the position of the sun was also incorporated in the calculations.

341.(a) The European was Thomas Roe.

342.(b)

343.(c)

344.(c) Surya, Pitamaha, Vasistha, Paulisa and Romaka.

345.(b)

346.(b)

347.(b) About 1400 B.C.

348.(a) All the planets were supposed to be in conjunction at the initial point of the celestial sphere after every 'Mahayuga'.

349.(a) 'Nakshatravidya'.

350.(c)

351.(a)

352.(b)

353.(b) The date varies from year to year.

354.(a) A solar calendar.

355.(b)

356.(c)

357.(b) and (d)

358.(b)

359.(a)

360.(b)

361.(d)

362.(d) Solar activity was at its peak then.

363.(b) At Brussels.

364.(c)

365.(d)

366.(d)

367.(c)

368.(b)

369.(b)

370.(a)

371.(a)

372.(c)

373.(b)

374.(a)

375.(d)

376.(c)

377.(d)

378.(a)

379.(b)

380.(d) However, their dates differ.

381.(b)

382.(c) John Milton is the author.

383.(a)

384.(a) First century Roman orator.

385.(d)

386.(b)

387.(a)

388.(a)

389.(c)

390.(b) Mercurial temperament.

391.(d) Earthly.

392.(a) Moony or Lunatic.

393.(c) Make hay while the sun shines.

394.(b) and (c) Meteoric or cometary rise.

395.(a)

396.(a)

397.(c) What is the good of a sundial in the shade?

398.(d)

399.(d) Thank your stars.

400.(a)

401.(b)

402.(d)

403.(c)

404.(b)

405.(a)

406.(b)

407.(b)

408.(b)

409.(b)

410.(b)

411.(c)

412.(c)

413.(a)

414.(d)

415.(c) Food not to be eaten during day.

416.(d)

417.(d)

418.(c)

419.(d) Often interpreted as 'breaking up of a star' – that's why evil. However, nowadays, Bollywood movies show this event as the auspicious time for wish fulfillment.

420.(b)

421.(a) Thanks to astrology.

422.(c)

423.(d)

424.(a) The Milky Way.

425.(b)

426.(b) Chandamama.

427.(a)

428.(c)

429.(b)

430.(a)

431.(b)

432.(c)

433.(d)

434.(a)

435.(c) Effelsberg Radio Telescope.

436.(d)

437.(b)

438.(d)

439.(b)

440.(c)

441.(d)

442.(a) Due to their tedious orbital calculations.

443.(b)

444.(c)

445.(a)

446.(d) William Herschel alone claimed the presence of solar inhabitants; the other two claimed that the sun was a planet.

447.(d)

448.(d)

449.(a)

450.(a)

451.(a) Designed by James W. Cadle.

452.(b)

453.(c)

454.(b)

455.(c)

456.(b)

457.(c) Dyson sphere is named after its conceiver, Freeman Dyson.

458.(a) and (d)

459.(b)

460.(c) and (d)
461.(a) Schiaparelli only reported the presence of 'canals'.
462.(a) Called 'Drake equation'.
463.(b)
464.(d)
465.(a)
466.(b)
467.(b)
468.(a) Marathwada district.
469.(a)
470.(b) At Kodaikanal.
471.(c)
472.(b) Called 'Vainu Bappu'.
473.(b) Narayangoan.
474.(b)
475.(c)
476.(c)
477.(d)
478.(b)
479.(a)
480.(a) New English School in 1954.
481.(c) Near Mumbai
482.(a)
483.(c)

484.(b)
485.(b)
486.(d)
487.(d)
488.(d)
489.(c)
490.(a)
491.(a)
492.(c)
493.(b)
494.(a)
495.(b)
496.(a)
497.(b)
498.(b)
499.(c)
500.(c)
501.(d)
502.(a)
503.(b)
504.(a) and (c)
505.(a)
506.(b)
507.(c) Originally in Marathi.
508.(b)
509.(c)
510.(d)
511.(a)
512.(c)
513.(a)

514.(b) An amateur Albert Jones also discovered the supernova.
515.(d)
516.(b)
517.(a)
518.(a) Frederich von Struve; Gustave von Struve; Karl von Struve; Otto von Struve; and Otto Wilhelm von Struve.
519.(c)
520.(d)
521.(a)
522.(d)
523.(a)
524.(d)
525.(d) In recent times, Landsat discovered the largest crater in Siberia.
526.(a)
527.(d)
528.(d)
529.(c)
530.(b)

531. The 3.81 metre primary mirror of the world's largest infrared telescope installed at Mauna Kea, Hawaii. The surface of the mirror is polished to provide surface accuracy within a tolerance of a few millions of centimetres.

532. An astrolabe used by mariners to determine latitude based on the observations of celestial objects. This piece is Arabic in origin.

533. Vacuum aluminising chamber at one Indian observatory, where mirrors of small telescopes are coated with a thin layer of aluminum needed for reflecting light. The layer is usually protected by a silicon coating to stand weather conditions.

534. It is the Infrared Astronomical Satellite (IRAS) launched in 1983 to study heavenly bodies in infrared light.

535. Coelostat, an instrument which follows the sun so that it could be studied.

536. The radio dishes of the Giant Meter-wave Radio Telescope installed near Pune. They are watching radio sources to messages from the outer space. It is the pride of Indian radio astronomy today.

SCORE YOURSELF!

Count the correct answers you have given and mark yourself as follows:

Average: if 425-449 answers are correct.

Good: if 450-474 answers are correct.

Excellent: if 475-499 answers are correct.

And if you score more than 500 correct, you are a **SUPER GENIUS** in astronomy!

www.ingramcontent.com/pod-product-compliance
Lightning Source LLC
Chambersburg PA
CBHW051346020726
47501CB00007B/2289